ALL THE BEFORES

SAMANTHA CHASE

All the Befores

Editor: Jillian Rivera

Cover Design: Uplifting Designs/Alyssa Garcia

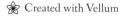 Created with Vellum

PRAISE FOR SAMANTHA CHASE

"Samantha Chase writes my kind of happily ever after!"

   -*NY Times & USA Today Bestselling Author* **Erin Nicholas**

"If you can't get enough of stories that get inside your heart and soul and stay there long after you've read the last page, then Samantha Chase is for you!"

   -*NY Times & USA Today Bestselling Author* **Melanie Shawn**

"A fun, flirty, sweet romance filled with romance and character growth and a perfect happily ever after."

   -*NY Times & USA Today Bestselling Author* **Carly Phillips**

"The openness between the lovers is refreshing, and their interactions are a balanced blend of sweet and spice. The planets may not have aligned, but the elements of this winning romance are definitely in sync."

   - ***Publishers Weekly, STARRED review***

"A true romantic delight, *A Sky Full of Stars* is one of the top gems of romance this year."

   - ***Night Owl Reviews, TOP PICK***

"Great writing, a winsome ensemble, and the perfect blend of heart and sass."

1

THE BIG HOUSE looked a little dark and sad tonight.

It fit her mood.

It wouldn't stay that way for long, though. Soon it was going to be filled with tons of people talking, laughing, loving, and celebrating.

But it was quiet right now. Tonight, Susannah Westbrook was the lone occupant of Magnolia on the Sound – her soon-to-be-open bed and breakfast – and she was the furthest she'd been in a long time to laughing, loving, and celebrating.

It didn't have to be this way...

And yet...it was.

A soft sigh escaped as she stood on the gravel driveway and marveled at the plantation-style home as she pushed her sad thoughts aside. The house represented hope to her. After what seemed like a lifetime of struggling – surviving a bad marriage, raising two kids on her own – she was finally feeling like her luck was changing. For years she had envisioned taking the house and turning it into something magnificent. It had been in her family for generations and now it was hers.

It was both exciting and bittersweet.

Her grandfather left it to her when he passed away a year ago and it had taken almost the entire year to make repairs from Hurricane Amelia as well as the renovations that would turn it from a family home into a B&B. It had been a labor of love and it was worth all the blood, sweat, and tears she put into it.

This was her dream – taking the old house and turning it into something magnificent; she wanted it to be the kind of place that showcased and celebrated a century of life and love in the South. For years she envisioned redecorating and making upgrades that would make it a showplace for anyone who walked through the massive double doors. Susannah had done her research and kept much of the historical feel to the home – including the family Bible and photos that showed not only Magnolia Sound when it was first founded, but also the family who first settled here. Walking around the house, anyone would feel the connection – the love – for the small coastal town. And when she opened the doors to her first guests next week, she couldn't wait to share all of that information and history with them.

She took one step toward the house when a light went on inside. Gasping, she froze. No one was supposed to be here. None of the lights were on timers and she had foolishly forgotten to turn any on before she'd left for her date earlier. Now what was she supposed to do?

Pulling her phone from her purse, she immediately pulled up her daughter Mallory's number. Because Mallory and her fiancé lived next door, Susannah hoped they would come over and check out what was going on inside the house with her.

The front door opened and the sound of a phone ringing wasn't just happening on the other end of the phone; it was happening...out on the front porch?

"Mallory?" she called out.

The front door opened farther and her daughter stepped out onto the porch as a light came on above her. "Hey, Mom! You're home early!"

Susannah practically sagged against her car. Pressing a hand over her heart, she forced herself to move and go up the front steps to greet Mallory. "What on earth are you doing here? You scared at least ten years off of my life when I saw a light go on inside."

Hugging her, Mallory laughed softly. "Sorry. I was going to bake some cookies to bring into the shop tomorrow, but I was low on ingredients."

"So you were raiding my pantry?"

"Guilty as charged," Mallory replied sheepishly. Arm in arm, they walked into the house. Closing the door behind her, Mallory looked at her mother and smiled broadly. "So? How was your night? Did you and Colton do anything exciting?"

"Oh, um...just dinner," she said, walking straight toward the kitchen.

"And...?" Mallory asked expectantly, almost as if she knew what had happened tonight.

Rather than answer right away, Susannah busied herself by putting a kettle on the stove to make some hot tea. She pulled two mugs down from the cabinets and tried to figure out a way to change the subject.

"Mom? Is everything all right?"

The last thing she wanted was to break down in front of her daughter, but it seemed like the events of the night were ready to catch up with her.

Bracing both hands on the cool granite countertop, Susannah hung her head as the first tears began to fall. "No," she sobbed. "Everything is all wrong."

In the blink of an eye, Mallory's arms were around her, embracing her. She didn't ask any questions. She simply held on as Susannah cried.

They stood there until the kettle began to whistle and Mallory reached out to turn it off before leading them over to the kitchen table to sit. Once Susannah was settled, Mallory went to make their tea and neither spoke until they each had a mug in front of them.

"I'm sorry I fell apart like that," Susannah began quietly, reaching for a napkin to wipe her face. "I didn't think it was going to hit me so hard."

For a moment, Mallory was silent, as if carefully considering her words. "What happened?"

Letting out a shuddery breath, she said, "Colton proposed tonight."

"Oh my goodness! That's amazing!"

"I turned him down."

"Oh...um...why? I thought you guys were...you know..."

"You wouldn't understand," Susannah said wearily. "Let's just say it's all for the best."

"Mom, I can't possibly say that while you're sitting here crying. How can it be for the best?"

"Just trust me, Mal, okay?" Resting her head in her hands, she wished they were discussing anything but this.

After several minutes, Mallory asked, "So then...that's it? You and Colton are through?"

She nodded.

It was another few minutes before Mallory said anything. "I get that you don't want to talk about this right now, but I also don't want you to be alone tonight. I'm going to stay and we can just sit and watch some TV or bake or you can go up to bed and I'll stay in one of the guest rooms and leave you be."

"Mal..."

Reaching across the table, Mallory placed one hand on top of hers. "I'm not leaving."

Emotion clogged her throat and all she could do was nod. Mallory pulled out her phone and stood, likely to call her fiancé to let him know where she was and what was going on. When she left the room to talk, Susannah was glad for the respite. She didn't let out an easy breath until Mallory's voice was barely audible.

Colton Hale had proposed to her.

And she had no idea it was coming.

None.

She was clueless when it came to relationships – always had been. Her ex-husband was her high-school sweetheart and they had gotten married right out of school because she was pregnant. When he left her, she put all of her time and energy into surviving and taking care of her children. Sam and Mallory were her entire world and she never even thought about dating until they were in college.

And boy had things changed in the dating world in those twenty years!

Still, Susannah hadn't found dating a necessity and she certainly never found someone who really piqued her interest.

Until Colton.

They had been dating for almost nine months now and even though she knew she was in love with him, there was no way she would even consider marrying him.

Or anyone.

No matter how much it broke her heart.

Pushing her cup of tea aside, she rested her face in her palms again. As she closed her eyes, she could still see the look of utter devastation on Colton's face when she turned him down. He was a good man – possibly the best man in the world – and that meant he deserved so much more than she could give him. He'd been married once before too and had no children so he didn't understand some of her reasons for turning him down. She did have children – well, grown children – but they always came first for her. Now Mallory was getting ready to get married, and Sam was going to get engaged any time now, so how could she possibly steal any of the spotlight from them? This was their time.

Hers was gone.

Long gone.

Now it was time for them to shine.

There was no way she was going to admit that to Mallory right now or possibly ever. She knew her daughter well enough to know she was fairly selfless and would claim it didn't matter, but it mattered to Susannah.

Not that it was her only reason for turning Colton down.

It seemed the list was endless.

He was five years younger than her; she was getting ready to start this new phase of her life with the B&B and that's where her focus needed to be. She was too old to be thinking about getting married again...

But more than anything, the words her ex-husband said to her so many years ago still plagued her.

You're not enough, Susannah. You've never been enough. No man is ever going to want you because you're lacking in so many ways.

Twenty years later and it still stung.

She didn't want to put Colton through that.

Right now, he thought he loved her and that she was enough. Well...he'd soon come to find out how wrong he was and then where would they be? It was better to end things now before they made a mistake.

Still...she missed him already.

Ached for him.

Oh, what she wouldn't give to be the kind of woman who...

"Okay, I talked to Jake and he knows I'm staying here tonight," Mallory said as she walked back into the room.

"You really didn't need to do that," Susannah said softly, staring down at the table. "I don't think I'm going to be too talkative tonight, Mal. It's too soon."

Sitting back down beside her, Mallory resumed her earlier position with her hand over her mother's. "And you don't need to talk about it. Not until you're ready. For the rest of the night, we'll find other things to do." She smiled when Susannah looked up at her. "Since I was planning on baking tonight, maybe we can do it together. You know you're going to need to start stocking up on baked good for when you have guests here."

As far as distractions went, it would work.

Still, there was a part of her that appreciated her daughter's attempt to help even though the other part really wanted to be alone to wallow in self-pity.

"Of course, if you're not into baking, I believe we can make popcorn and turn on something on Netflix while we just lounge in the new library. How about *Dirty Dancing* or *Pretty Woman*? I know those are a few of your favorites." Mallory paused. "What do you think?"

"Oh, sweetheart, I don't know. I'm really not the best company right now..."

Mallory squeezed her hand. "If you really want me to

leave, I will. But I want you to know that the thought of you being here alone while you're feeling like this is killing me. You've gotten me through some really rough breakups..."

"Jake was the only one who really broke your heart," Susannah clarified. "And in the end, it all worked out."

As she said the words, she realized how there was the potential for her daughter to turn that around and use it on her.

Luckily, she didn't.

"Still, just...humor me. Please. Go put on your jammies and meet me back here. Even if you don't need cookies for future guests, I want them for the shop tomorrow." She stood and smiled. "And I promise to replenish all the ingredients I use so I don't leave you lacking."

It was pointless to keep arguing. The truth of the matter was that her daughter was worried about her and wanted to be here to help. It was incredibly sweet and, instead of being a brat, Susannah knew she should embrace this because they didn't often get time like this together.

Even though there was a broken heart involved.

Standing, she reached out and pulled Mallory into her arms and hugged her, placing a soft kiss on her cheek. "Thank you for understanding." When she pulled back, she did her best to smile. "Give me a few minutes to go change and wash my face and I'll be back to help with the cookies."

"I'll get everything started," Mallory said with a smile of her own.

Susannah turned to walk away when something hit her. "Oh, and uh...Mallory?"

"Yeah?"

"No eating the cookie dough without me."

She heard her daughter's laughter as she walked out of the room and it eased some of her heartache.

Colton Hale was normally an optimistic man.

Some would say overly optimistic.

Not tonight.

It was after midnight and he was sitting alone in his tiny beach bungalow with dozens of nearly burned out candles and one small lamp on while he stared at the diamond engagement ring in his hand.

Susannah had turned him down.

In every scenario he had played out in his mind, not once did she turn him down. Sure there were a few where she was a little hesitant, but he always won her over. Lord knew the woman could be stubborn, but he'd never seen her behave the way she did tonight. It was as if he had proposed to a stranger.

And it just about gutted him.

How was he supposed to move on from this? Sure, he'd been married before and survived a divorce, but by the time he and Dana decided to call it quits, it was a relief for both of them. Ten years of marriage and they had become polite strangers who were just ready not to be with each other anymore. It had stung, sure, but it was nothing compared to the hurt he felt right now.

How was that for crazy?

He had planned this night for a month, had done everything right – including going to Sam and Mallory to get their blessings.

Which they had given him.

For the night itself, Colton filled the place with Susannah's favorite flowers – tulips. He bought her favorite wine – a pink Moscato – to go with the steaks he was going to grill for dinner. Everything was perfect. When she arrived at his house, he took one look at her and simply couldn't believe how lucky he was. From the very first time he saw her when she moved back to Magnolia Sound three years ago, he was smitten. It had taken him years to get up the courage to talk to her and ask her out, but it only took one date to know she was it for him.

And he really thought she felt the same about him.

Man did it suck to be wrong.

He had gotten down on one knee and everything – had thought he was being the most romantic man in the world. With the ring in his hand, he professed his love to Susannah and then watched as her expression went from confusion to pure horror. She looked at the ring like it were a serpent rather than a gift.

The thing was, he knew she was scared – he saw it on her face once she forced herself to look at him. There had never been any secrets between them and there were two things that were clear from day one. First, Sam and Mallory were her world. And second, her ex-husband had done a real number on her. He didn't just leave; he was cruel leading up to it and then dumped all the responsibility of raising two children on her while he moved on without them. She didn't talk about her ex much, but when she did, it was never anything positive – except to say that without him she wouldn't have her children.

Children, he thought with a small laugh. Sam and Mallory were both adults in healthy relationships and were both going to be married within a year. If anything, Colton thought the timing to propose was perfect. With the two of them settled, he thought Susannah would be ready for something for herself.

Just another way he was sorely mistaken.

Raking a hand through his graying hair, he let out a long

breath. It was obvious he was clueless and maybe Susannah was right to turn him down. If he had no idea how she felt and had gotten so many things wrong, what the hell kind of husband could he possibly be?

One that loved her completely.

Clearly love wasn't enough.

Not in this particular situation.

It was late and he was so tired – not that he thought he was going to get much sleep tonight. Thoughts of everything that transpired would undoubtedly haunt him. Still, he couldn't stay sitting in this chair. Looking around the small space he called home, there were remnants of what should have been a celebration.

Now they just mocked him.

Rising, he let out another sigh. The first thing he did was walk over to his dining room table, pick up the ring box and lovingly place the diamond solitaire back inside. The sound of the box shutting was almost as loud as gunfire. Walking from the room, he placed the box in his bedside table, staring hard at it before slowly closing the drawer.

That was one thing down.

Walking back out to the living room, he felt overwhelmed but forced himself to keep moving. As he went, he blew out the dozens of candles he had lit to make the house seem more romantic.

Lots of good that did for him.

Next, he cleaned up the dinner dishes and cleaned the kitchen. Then he made sure the dining table was wiped down. For the most part, everything was now back in its place and it looked like it did before Susannah arrived earlier except for one thing...

He had to figure out what to do with dozens of tulips.

2

"If you even think of eating that, I will punch you."

Sam Westbrook looked at his twin sister and frowned. "Mal, it is way too early for this. I came over like you asked and now you're telling me I'm not allowed to eat any of the donuts I bought? What the hell?"

Rolling her eyes, Mallory moved the box of pastries out of his reach. "You need to keep your voice down. Mom's still sleeping."

Slouching slightly in his seat at the kitchen table, Sam asked, "What's going on? You didn't say much in your text last night."

"I don't know much," she began and then punched her brother in the arm when he started to snicker. "Grow up."

Sighing dramatically, he straightened. "Okay, what do you know?"

"Colton proposed and she turned him down," she said sadly. "I don't get it. They've been inseparable and I know she's crazy about him..."

"There's a difference between being crazy about someone and wanting to marry them," he countered.

"Although, I have to admit, I really thought she would have said yes."

"Exactly. They were always so happy whenever we saw them together. And when Colton told us his plan to propose, it seemed like a no-brainer. How could Mom turn it down? I mean, I don't know what went wrong!"

"Well what did she say when you guys talked last night?"

"That's just it. She didn't want to talk. She said she wasn't ready and I stayed because I couldn't stand the thought of her being alone." She paused. "Honestly, I thought she would have caved at some point and started to talk about it, but she never did."

He looked at her like she was crazy. "So what did the two of you do? Just sit around and stare at each other?"

Rolling her eyes, Mallory explained, "We watched a couple of her favorite movies. It seemed to help."

"Oh, God...*Dirty Dancing*?" he asked with a small laugh.

She nodded. "Followed by *The Princess Bride*."

"Ugh...better you than me." He paused. "I'd say she's a private person, but once she started dating Colt, she seemed to open up more. You have no idea how many nights I came home here and had uncomfortable conversations with her about their relationship." He shuddered. "It was beyond awkward. And that's not counting the mornings I found them half dressed in here making breakfast."

"Oh, stop. You're an adult. Deal with it."

"Easy for you to say. You weren't the one begging Mom to put on some pants," he said.

"Okay, this is getting us nowhere..."

"Look, until we know why she turned him down, everything is just speculation. And if she's upset, the last thing we should be doing is pushing her to talk."

"How can you say that? If we don't get her to talk, we can't make her feel better or possibly convince her she made a mistake!"

Sam simply stared at her before yawning loudly.

"Okay, fine. So where does that leave us?" Mallory demanded, feeling more than a little annoyed with her brother's take on the situation.

"We wait for her to get up and take our cues from there. In the meantime, we have a couple of donuts and maybe a cup of coffee."

"For the love of it, could you please focus on something other than your stomach!" Shoving the box of donuts at him, she snapped, "You know what? Here. Go ahead! Eat! Be selfish! See if I care!"

With an easy grin, he opened the box. "Don't mind if I do!"

"There better be one of Mrs. Henderson's apple crullers in that box for me," Susannah said as she walked into the room. She yawned broadly and squinted against the bright sunlight streaming into the kitchen. It had been a long time since she'd walked in and found both her children sitting at the breakfast table, and it made her smile.

"There are two," Sam confirmed.

Mallory jumped to her feet. "Why don't you sit, Mom, and I'll make us all some coffee, okay?"

Nodding, Susannah shuffled toward the table and kissed Sam on the head before taking her seat. "I'd ask what you're doing here so early, but I'm pretty sure I already know the answer."

"Mom..." Mallory started.

"We're just worried about you," Sam said. "I wanted to

see for myself that you were okay and see if there was anything I can do."

It was too early to start crying again and rather than risk it, she reached into the pastry box and pulled out a cruller and took a bite. From the corner of her eye she saw her son's knowing smirk.

They sat in silence for several minutes until Mallory walked back over with coffee for all of them. Once she sat, Susannah knew she needed to say something; otherwise they'd sit here and stare at her with worry.

Taking a sip of her coffee, she let out a satisfied moan. When she looked up, they were both watching her warily. "Okay, look, I get it. You're both concerned and I love you for it. However, I'm just not sure what I'm supposed to say here."

The twins exchanged looks and Sam spoke first. "We thought you and Colt were happy together."

She nodded and cradled the coffee mug in her hands. "We were."

"You've never mentioned having a fight," Mallory commented.

"We never did."

"Then what's this about, Mom?" Sam asked gently. "Because from where we're sitting, you should be celebrating right now."

Shifting slightly in her seat, Susannah took a minute to collect her thoughts. "I guess...I mean, I never thought... it's just..." Her eyes welled with tears and her voice cracked.

Sam reached over and took one of her hands in his. "If you're not ready to talk about this, it's okay."

But she waved him off. "No, the sooner we all talk about it, the sooner I can move on."

"Is that what you want to do?" Mallory asked. "Move on?"

Nodding, Susannah wiped away some stray tears. "I never planned on getting married again," she said firmly, staring down at the table. "It wasn't something I wanted to do or something I even thought about. I was happy to be dating Colton but that's all I thought we were doing. I had no idea he wanted more."

"O-kay, but...is that really so bad?" Mallory asked carefully. "Just because you never *planned* on getting married again doesn't mean you can't think about it now. Did he refuse to give you time to think about it?"

Susannah shook her head.

"Then..."

But Sam interrupted her. "Mom, I get why you never thought about getting married again – I do. Dad was the worst and it left you with a bad taste in your mouth about marriage. On top of that, you were too busy raising us to think about it. But now...I mean, maybe you do need to think about it. Colton's a great guy – and believe me, it hurts to say that because I didn't want to like him."

She knew he was trying to make light of the situation, but if anything, it made her feel worse. Colton was a really great guy. He had shown her that not all men were mean and careless – that some men could be trusted and loving. He was everything she never knew existed and he made her feel things she didn't know she could feel.

And yet, here we are...

"I know you struggled in the beginning, sweetheart, and it meant a lot when you accepted our relationship and developed a friendship with Colton. It meant a lot to him, too."

"So I can understand you not being keen on marriage

because of Dad," Mallory went on, "but that situation had nothing to do with you. That was all him, Mom. You know that, right? Dad was the reason your marriage failed. Not you."

"It takes two people to make a marriage work," Susannah said, her voice trembling slightly. "And it takes two people for it to fail. I'm not blameless in what went wrong."

"Yes, you are," Sam said defiantly. "You did everything for all of us! You did everything for Dad – you were a great wife and a great mother and he didn't appreciate any of it. Do *not* for even one minute try to take the blame for what happened."

She loved how he jumped to her defense – he always had. She squeezed his hand and forced herself to look up and smile at him. "You were so young when your father left and you don't know everything that happened."

"But…"

"Believe me, I'm putting a solid ninety-five percent of the blame on your father, but I wasn't perfect either."

"I don't buy that," Mallory said, taking Susannah's other hand in hers.

"Guys…"

"So if it's just the fact that you're not ready to get married, then why did you break up?" Sam asked.

"How do you know we broke up?"

The look he gave her said, "Really?"

"Okay, fine. We broke up." She sighed. "I didn't think it was fair to him to stay in a relationship when we both want different things."

They all sat in silence for several minutes, each lost in their own thoughts, sipping their coffee and eating donuts. It was nice. It was comfortable.

"If your marriage to Dad had ended differently – like with him not taking off and being a selfish jerk," Mallory began, "do you think you'd still look at being married the same way?"

She shrugged. "Who can say?"

"C'mon, Mom. It sounds to me like you're still letting Dad influence you and that's not right," Sam commented. "And if that's all this is about..."

"It's not..."

Both kids groaned.

"So what happens now?" Mallory asked.

Susannah took another long sip of her coffee before responding. "Well, honestly, I have a lot on my plate. The inn has its first guests next week, Christmas is three weeks away, we still have to work on your wedding plans," she said, looking at Mallory. "You know you really need to get serious about this. You've been procrastinating on setting a date, but once the inn is open for booking full-time after the first of the year, we may have a hard time finding a date for you to have the wedding here."

"Yeah, I know..."

"Please tell me you're not procrastinating because you have issues with marriage too," Sam grumbled.

"*What?!* That's ridiculous!" Mallory cried. "Why would you even think that?"

He looked between her and their mother and then back again. "Um...pot? Meet kettle."

"That's not even remotely the case," Mallory argued.

"Really? Then why haven't you set a date? Seems to me you've been wanting to marry Jake since you were eighteen. And now that he's asked and you accepted, you're in no rush to actually do it!"

Mallory frowned. "You don't know what you're talking

about, Sam. I don't see *you* rushing to put a ring on Shelby's finger."

"Are you kidding me?" he said with a laugh. "If it were up to me, we'd be married already!"

"Seriously?"

He nodded. "It was going to be a surprise, but...I've got the ring and I plan on proposing on Christmas Eve."

"Maybe she won't say yes," Mallory said tartly, giving him a smirk as she picked up her coffee.

"Mallory!" Susannah cried. "That is a terrible thing to say!"

"And in really bad taste considering the current circumstances," Sam added and seemed pleased when his sister paled. Clearing his throat, he sat up a little taller, and definitely looked smug.

"Okay, this is getting us nowhere," Susannah declared, standing up. "You'll set the date when you're ready and, in the meantime, I have the inn to keep me busy." She turned to put her coffee cup in the sink when Mallory called out to her. "Hmm?"

"Just answer one more thing and I promise to let this go."

Somehow she doubted it, but she nodded anyway.

"Do you love him?"

Colton's face instantly sprang to mind and her heart squeezed tight. Tears stung her eyes and all she could do was nod again.

"Oh, Mom..." In the blink of an eye, both Sam and Mallory were on their feet and hugging her. She simply stood there and let them and considered herself the luckiest mother in the world to have two such caring children. After a few minutes, she excused herself to go take a shower.

Once Mallory heard the door to the family wing close,

she turned to Sam. "You know we have to do something, right?"

"Mal, what are we supposed to do? She seems pretty set on moving on."

"Did she?"

He frowned. "Um..."

"There were a lot of flimsy excuses in there but at the end, she admitted that she loved Colton. There's still hope!"

"It's really not our place..."

She punched him in the arm. "Just...leave it to me. I'm going to go home and talk to Jake. Considering Colton works for him, I'm sure he can get some insight into how he feels about the breakup."

"How do you think he feels, Mal? He proposed and got turned down. I can pretty much guarantee he's not feeling great."

"Don't be so snarky," she snapped. "I think we give them both today to let things sink in and then Monday Jake will talk to him." She paused. "Or..."

"Oh, no," Sam said, taking a step back. "I am not going to be the one to go talk to Colt. Nuh-uh. No way."

"Come on, Sam! Don't you care that Mom's hurting?"

"Of course I care! I wouldn't be here if I didn't!"

"Then won't you please..."

He held up a hand to stop her. "If I do it, it will be when I want and how I want. You are not going to dictate it to me. Deal?"

She smiled sweetly up at him. "Deal."

———

"Jake? What are you doing here?"

It was a stupid question. Colton knew exactly why his boss and friend was here.

He was just embarrassed that he felt the need to come check on him.

Jake Summerford stood on Colton's front porch looking a little uncomfortable even as he offered a small smile. "Mind if I come in?"

Stepping aside, Colton motioned for him to step inside and once they were in, he offered Jake something to drink.

"Thanks, but I'm good," Jake said, taking a seat. Once Colton was seated on the sofa opposite him, Jake gave him another small smile. "You doing okay?"

Why lie?

"No," he said glumly. "Not really."

Jake nodded. "Mallory told me what happened. I mean, not everything, just...well...that you proposed and..."

"And Susannah turned me down and broke up with me." He paused. "Yeah."

Leaning forward, resting his elbows on his knees, Jake let out a long breath. "I'll be honest with you, Colt. I'm not even sure what to say."

"I'm still a little dumbfounded myself."

"If you need some time off or...anything," Jake offered, "just say the word. I know this can't be easy for you."

"Thanks." He paused and knew what he needed to ask if he was going to have any peace. "How is she?"

"I didn't see or talk to her. Mallory stayed over at the house last night and Sam was over with them this morning."

"They're good kids," he said solemnly. "They mean the world to Susannah."

"And she means the world to them," Jake replied. "For what it's worth, Colt, Mallory said Susannah's hurting too. You have to know the decision wasn't easy for her."

All he could do was nod.

"You know she didn't have a great marriage..."

"It was over twenty years ago," he argued, but there was no heat behind his words. "She's an amazing woman who has overcome so much and she has this amazing future in front of her with the inn, then you and Mallory getting married, and I'm sure Sam's not far behind. I don't get why she keeps looking back at something that clearly only made her stronger."

Jake didn't seem to have a response to that.

"I know I probably should have thought all of this through – maybe should have felt her out a little to see how she felt about marriage. I just never thought her first marriage would still be an issue."

"Yeah, I get that," Jake agreed. "But sometimes it's not an issue until...you know...something like this comes up. Maybe she just got spooked. Maybe you guys should take a couple of days and then sit down and talk again."

It was something Colton had thought about while lying in bed last night, but he shot it down because he didn't feel strong enough to face rejection from her a second time.

With a shrug he said, "I don't know. Maybe."

"It's something to think about." Jake studied his hands for a moment. "But seriously, Colt, is there anything I can do for you? Anything you need?"

"Right now, I don't know. I think my head's still spinning a bit. It's like I don't even know what to do with myself. For almost a year, Susannah and I have seen each other every day. As a matter of fact, we were supposed to go to the big warehouse store down in Wilmington today to do the final shopping for the inn's pantry." He shook his head and looked up at Jake. "The thought of not seeing her or talking to her again is just...it's killing me."

"Well, it's not like you'll *never* see Susannah again. Magnolia's a small community and..."

"It's not the same and you know it. Running into her in the grocery store or seeing her across the street while walking around in town isn't what I'm looking for." Standing, he began to pace. "I don't know if I can stay here, Jake. I don't know if I can handle what happens from here."

Rising, Jake walked over and put a hand on his shoulder to calm him. "Don't make any rash decisions just yet. Like I said, take a few days to let everything settle in. You've lived here your entire life and you didn't move after your divorce, so you know you can do this."

"Again, it's not the same. When my marriage ended, there weren't any hard feelings. Dana and I had simply grown apart. And besides, she moved away."

"Oh."

Stepping away, Colton moved to stare out the front window – practically willing Susannah to show up and say she'd made a mistake. Hands in his pockets, he knew it wasn't going to happen. "I just want you to know that I'd give you plenty of notice," he said solemnly. "Like I wouldn't just pack up and leave without telling you." Looking over his shoulder, he offered Jake a weak smile. "You've always been a good friend and a fair boss. I won't leave you hanging."

"Colt, that is the last thing on my mind. I'm worried about you – as a friend. The work stuff doesn't mean squat right now, okay?"

He nodded.

They stood there, side by side staring out the window when someone pulled into the driveway. Beside him, he heard Jake chuckle but Colton had no idea why. Without a word, he stepped around him and went to open the front door while he waited.

A minute later, Sam came strolling up the front path – his hair in disarray and looking all kinds of intimidating.

Until he was standing a few feet away.

Then he smiled.

And then that smile grew when he spotted Jake in the doorway too.

Stepping up to the door, he handed Colton a box from the local bakery and wished them both a good morning before clapping his hands together and saying, "Gentlemen, let's do some damage control!"

3

For two days Susannah did her best to keep busy. There was so much to do to get ready for the inn's first official guests that she almost didn't have time to let her thoughts go to how much she missed Colton.

The nights were a completely different story.

And unfortunately, right now she was dealing with a bull in a china shop who wanted to do nothing but talk about all that had gone wrong.

"Honestly, Susannah, this is for the best," Georgia Bishop, Susannah's cousin, said as she moved around and fussed with the silk flower arrangement in the inn's library. "Don't you have enough on your plate without having to deal with a needy man?"

"I never said Colton was needy..."

"I mean, look at all the work you've put into this house! Almost an entire year has been spent renovating and rebuilding and if you don't keep your focus, well...the whole thing could fail. And then where will you be?"

"It's not going to fail, Georgia."

Her cousin's expression pinched slightly. "Most new

businesses fail, Susannah. You have to be shrewd and you need to maintain your focus. As it is, you'll be distracted by Mallory's wedding plans and then if Sam decides to get married, you'll be involved in that too, I'm sure." She paused. "Of course, Mason and Scarlett want something different when they get married so you won't have to be involved in that."

Georgia's son and his fiancé were expecting their first baby together and everyone had been wondering when they were going to get married. "Any news on that front? Have they set a date?" Susannah asked, hoping to get the focus off of herself and on to Georgia's children.

Sighing dramatically, she straightened a silk lily before turning to sit on the sofa. "Beau and I offered to pay for a wedding for them – you know, since Scarlett comes from such a poor family – but they just won't commit to anything. It's very frustrating. I've got the country club on speed dial just in case. We would love to host a reception there. It would be so elegant."

Forcing a smile, she nodded.

"But I suppose with the holidays being right around the corner, it's the last thing on their minds. I'm sure if I wait until after the new year, they'll have decided." Then she frowned. "Of course, then Scarlett will be well-advanced in her pregnancy and she's already mentioned not wanting to deal with dress shopping or trying to find one that will fit." Another pause while she shook her head. "Although, who can blame her? It seems rather tacky to be wearing a virginal white gown when she's clearly expecting a child. She might feel ridiculous."

"You never know," Susannah said pleasantly.

"So you see, Susannah, you've really dodged a bullet by

turning Colton down. You don't want to have to worry about all those silly wedding details. Especially at your age."

"Um...excuse me?"

"Hmm?"

"What was that supposed to mean – *especially at my age?*" she demanded, trying to hold on to her anger.

"I'm just saying...just like Scarlett not wanting to wear a white gown while six or seven months pregnant, you might not want to wear one when you're...you know...almost fifty," Georgia said in her perfect little southern drawl and her stiff smile.

"First of all, I'm only forty-six. And secondly, getting married doesn't mean I have to wear a traditional wedding gown," she argued. "But if I did, it would be my decision and mine alone!"

To her credit, her cousin merely arched a blonde brow at her. "So if it's not the fear of looking ridiculous for being a bride at your age, why aren't you marrying that man?"

With a weary sigh, Susannah sat down at the other end of the sofa. "I never said it had anything to do with how I'd look as a bride, Georgia. That would be the most absurd reason not to get married."

"Then what *is* the reason? I would think after the way you've been courting attention here in town the last few years that getting married would be right up your alley."

Every time she thought she and her cousin could get along, Georgia opened her mouth and said something like this. Susannah thought she'd be used to it by now, but right now it was like the straw that broke the camel's back. She'd done her best to hold it together ever since she drove away from Colton's house – partly for her own sake, but partly because she didn't want anyone worrying about her. But something in her cousin's condescending tone pushed her last button.

Slowly, she turned her head. "Courting attention? *Courting* attention?" she repeated for emphasis. "How exactly have I done that, Georgia?"

But before Georgia could even answer, Susannah was on her feet and towering over her cousin.

"I had always planned on moving back to Magnolia! I grew up in this town! I have friends and family here! It's not my fault that you can't stand sharing the attention!"

"Don't be ridiculous…"

Susannah wasn't even listening. "That's what this is about, isn't it? It's what it's always about! *You!* You seriously can't be happy or even feel compassion toward anyone because all you can do is think about yourself and how these situations affect you!"

"Honestly, Susannah, you're not even making sense," Georgia said with mild annoyance.

"You loved having all the attention on you as some sort of matriarch in the family when I wasn't here. It was all fine and well when I was only here for a few weeks in the summer but once I was back for good, your bitch-factor went off the charts!"

"My…my…what?"

Leaning down, Susannah said, "Bitch. Factor." Straightening, she paced a few feet away. "You were upset that I got the house, you've been snippy and condescending about Mallory's wedding and trying to convince her to have something small so you'll be able to outdo it when your girls get married!"

"Now you're just talking gibberish, Susannah."

"Am I?" she demanded. "You can't stand that Mallory's wedding is going to be a big deal in this town. And you've made more than enough faces over the fact that Sam and Shelby will more than likely follow suit quickly. So you must be positively *giddy* that I turned Colton down because now you can hold *that* failure over my head! Well...shame on you!"

"Don't you have enough?" Georgia snapped, her own patience ending. Coming to her feet, she did her best to look intimidating. "Yes, you got the house, and yes, your children have their lives together and are getting married. And for months you've paraded around town in total bliss with Colton! Not everyone has it like that, Susannah! And not everyone can handle having all that love and...and...all that happiness thrown in their face!"

For a moment, all Susannah could do was blink.

"Um...what are you talking about?"

Georgia's eyes went wide for a moment before she turned away, searching for her purse. She picked it up and went to scurry from the room. "It's nothing. Just...nothing."

Susannah didn't let her get far. At the grand foyer, she stopped her cousin. "Georgia, talk to me! What is going on?"

And for the first time ever, she saw tears in her cousin's eyes.

"You don't realize how much you have, Susannah," Georgia said quietly, primly. "Before you moved here, I thought I had everything. Then I saw the way you interact with Sam and Mallory and...and everyone you meet. People smile when they see you – they seek you out. People see me coming and walk away."

"That's not entirely true. I saw the article in the paper about the work you're doing with the animal rescue. It looked like all those puppies were very happy to be running around you."

Georgia rolled her eyes. "They're just dogs, Susannah."

"Animals are known for being excellent judges of character," she said, hoping to make light of the conversation.

"My girls don't reach out to me the way Mallory does to you," she went on. "And Mason went for weeks without talking to me." Swiping tears away, she went on. "I can't remember the last time Beau looked at me the way Colton looked at you."

Her heart squeezed hard as the image came to her mind.

"I...I wished for something like this to happen."

Susannah stared at her in confusion. "What does that mean?"

"It means...I wished for something to happen to cause you some of the pain and misery I was feeling," she replied, her voice small. "And now that it's happened, I feel terrible."

Some of the fight went out of Susannah but not all of it. "Well you should. That's a terrible thing to wish on someone. For all your bitchy ways, I just wished for you to get nicer and maybe unclench a bit."

Georgia looked away and Susannah could see the flush of embarrassment on her face, but that didn't stop her from continuing. She'd waited too long to get this off her chest. "I've never been rude to you and I always tried to be friendly with you, but you've always kept me at arm's length. After a while, I just stopped trying. But right now, I need people around me who care that I'm hurting, not cheering because of it." When she turned to walk away, Georgia called her back. "What?" she snapped.

"I'm sorry, Susannah. Truly. I...I know what it's like to be in a relationship that isn't working. I'm sorry you had to go through that with Colton."

Her shoulders sagged sadly. "That's just it, Georgia. The relationship *was* working."

"Then I don't understand. Why did you break up?"

And then Susannah saw something else she'd never seen before from her cousin.

Concern.

Tears stung her eyes and she realized how utterly ridiculous the two of them must look, but she didn't care. "I got scared," she admitted, her voice cracking. "I've already had a failed marriage and know I'm a terrible wife. Why would I go there again?"

If anything, Georgia's expression went from concerned to shock. "Why would you think you're a terrible wife?" She made a tsking sound before stepping in closer. "You did everything you could possibly do for that man, Susannah, and we all know it. You are not the reason your marriage failed."

And in a very un-Georgia-like move, she hugged Susannah.

Hard.

"It must have killed you to just admit that to me," she teased and was relieved when Georgia laughed and simply hugged her tighter.

It was a good moment.

Maybe even a great one.

Turning, they walked arm in arm back to the living room and talked about what they were both going to do next.

———

There was a definite chill in the air and as Colton held his travel mug of hot coffee, he did his best to focus on the task in front of him.

He had taken Jake's advice and took a couple of days off from work to get his head together. Today was his first day back and he took a moment to stare at the construction site in front of him. It wasn't a huge job – Coleman Construction was handling the renovations on a new boat storage facility at the Magnolia Yacht Club – and he had a small crew to watch over, but he supposed it was the right place for him to be right now.

Taking a step away from his truck, he was about to go double check the lumber that was delivered while he wasn't here yesterday when his phone rang.

"What's up, Jake?" he said when he answered.

"Hey, Colt. I was just going over some paperwork and saw we were shorted some materials on your job. I need you to do a quick inventory for me so I can make some calls and get what we're missing out to you ASAP."

"Can do. Give me about an hour. I'll get everyone to help."

"You've got four guys with you today, right?"

"Yup." He took a sip of his coffee. "Why? You want to send me more?"

"Actually, I was thinking of pulling two for the next couple of days. We've got an issue with the inn and I need a crew over there."

"What's going on?" he asked, concern for Susannah instantly filling him.

He heard Jake mutter a curse. "It's nothing major. Just a few things the new city inspector noticed and he's threatening to stop Susannah from opening next week. Nothing a few guys can't handle."

"Dammit, Jake! That's just not possible! Everything was perfect at the inn! I saw to it myself!"

"Look, Colt, no one's blaming you for anything. This guy's new and just being a bit nit-picky, if you know what I mean. Still, I don't want to risk the inn missing its opening over some minor stuff. So maybe you can just send..."

"No," he said adamantly. "I was there from day one of those renovations and I know every inch of the place practically like the back of my hand. If there's work to be done there, I'll do it."

Jake was silent for a moment. "You sure you want to do that? I mean, it could be awkward. You're going to have to work with Susannah a bit. I don't know if the two of you have spoken since...well...you know."

"We haven't but I don't think now's the time to worry about that. The inn is Susannah's dream and I'm not going to let anyone ruin that for her!"

"Okay, okay...if you're sure you're all right with it, then..."

"I am."

"Just get me that inventory and..."

"My guys are on it. I'll have Jim Connelly lead it up and let him know you need those numbers within the hour. Once I get them set up, I'll head over to Susannah's."

"If you're sure..."

"I said I was!" he snapped as he hung up. As soon as his phone was back in his pocket, he cursed himself. Mouthing off to his boss was probably not the smartest thing to do. Still, there was no way he would trust anyone else to go over to the inn to do any kind of work. That place was his baby and not just because it was Susannah's. He'd been one of the first ones on site after Hurricane Amelia damaged the house and the property and he had been on site for every day of the work from beginning to end. His mind reeled as he tried to imagine just what could be wrong.

"Probably should have gotten that information before I opened my damn mouth," he muttered as he walked over to talk to his crew.

After giving them their instructions and placing Jim in charge, Colton was in his truck and fighting a panic attack at the thought of seeing Susannah.

It was too soon and not something he was mentally prepared for. If anything, he had figured it would be well after the holidays before they would potentially cross paths.

And he had foolishly volunteered to not only see her but put himself in a position where he'd have to be around her for at least a day or two.

"I'm a damn fool."

Yeah, but he was a responsible one and he knew he couldn't hide forever.

This was clearly going to be his new normal – life where he wasn't dating or marrying Susannah – so he might as well pull the bandage off and deal with it.

As he drove across town, a thought hit him – when Sam had shown up at his place on Sunday and mentioned coming up with an excuse to get Colton over to the inn, he had shot him down. There was no way he wanted some flimsy excuse to make him look like some sort of clingy man. It was one thing if Susannah didn't love him; it was another if she lost all respect for him too.

All this meant was that the work for the inn was legit.

But it still brought him back to the conversation with Sam.

After shooting down all the excuses to bring him and Susannah together, they had left it that Sam wasn't giving up and was willing to do whatever it took to see his mother happy.

And if he already didn't think Sam was a good man, that attitude pretty much cemented it for him.

The one thing Colton had to remind himself was that Susannah's happiness didn't necessarily have anything to do with him.

Not anymore.

And that was something he couldn't allow himself to dwell on as he pulled into the long, gravel drive that led to the inn. Once he was parked, he simply sat there and stared up at the house for several minutes as he tried to figure out what he was supposed to do and say when Susannah opened the door. How was he supposed to go back to being casual acquaintances when all he wanted to do was turn back the clock and go back to the way they were before he proposed? How was he going to just talk about carpentry repairs when he knew he was going to want to hold her and kiss her and be with her? How could he possibly…

A loud knock on the truck window made him jump and brought him out of his reverie.

Susannah.

Holding up his hand, he grabbed his clipboard and opened the door. Once he was standing beside her and felt like he could speak, he cleared his throat and forced a smile. "Hey, Susannah."

Her smile was a little shy – and completely endearing – as she combed her hair behind her ear. "Hey, Colt. What are you...?" She paused and noticed the clipboard in his hands. "I um...I didn't realize you were the one who was going to come and look over the repairs the city is insisting I make."

With a curt nod, he focused on the house rather than

looking at her because it hurt too much. Just days ago, he would have been allowed to lean in and kiss her hello before taking her by the hand and walking up to the front porch. Now he had to keep a respectable distance, act professional, and remember why he was here.

"Jake didn't mention what the issue was, but I have to admit that I'm confused. We passed all inspections. It was a done deal. Why was anyone even out here at this point?"

"It's my own fault, really. I was down at town hall because I was meeting Mason and Scarlett for lunch. We were going to go over some of the social media campaigns Scarlett's planning for the inn."

He nodded.

"We were standing around and talking in Mason's office and I mentioned how I'd like to host larger events in the spring and summer," she explained, "You know, utilizing the new deck and the gardens."

He nodded again.

"Anyway, out of nowhere, this guy walked in and mentioned overhearing the conversation and said that the deck needed to be rated for commercial use and I'd need to add more lighting!"

"But...how would he even...?"

"I know, right? So Mason tried talking to him and this guy was insistent on coming over and inspecting everything since it seemed like this was a new idea."

"He really had no right..."

"I have to admit, Mason really tried to smooth things over, but this guy..." She groaned. "He was just the worst. I was so upset that I told Scarlett we'd have to reschedule lunch and our meeting and I had this...this...jerk follow me home so we could just get the whole thing over with."

"Damn, Susannah. I don't even know what to..."

"And as if all that wasn't upsetting enough, he gets done inspecting the deck, walked through the house on his way out, and claimed that the grading on the driveway was not sufficient nor was the space allotted for parking!" Reaching out, she placed a hand on his arm. He knew it wasn't anything personal – she wasn't touching him for any other reason except she was upset. But still, it took him a minute to focus on what she was saying and not on how good her hands felt on him.

"These aren't small or quick fixes, are they? I mean, the grounds have already been landscaped! I can't dig up the whole front yard and have it fixed by Friday, Colton! What am I going to do?"

Next thing he knew, he had his arms full of Susannah and it was a long time before either of them let go.

4

Okay, maybe it had been a mistake to fall apart like that, but as Susannah made Colton a fresh cup of coffee while he was on the phone arguing with someone over these new coding issues, she couldn't find the will to care. Her feelings for him hadn't gone away or even changed, but their relationship was just...different now.

He stormed into the kitchen and right out to the deck, arguing the entire time about permits and codes and materials. She had to smile because the man seemed to remember every single detail of what went into the work here on the inn and she knew right now that gave him the advantage.

Well, at least she hoped it did.

Unsure of what to do with herself in the meantime, she wiped down the countertops and then placed his coffee on the kitchen table. Hopefully he'd see it when he came back in.

With nothing left to do, she walked out of the room and to her own apartment. She had converted what had originally been her grandfather's master suite and two guest rooms into a two-bedroom, two-bathroom apartment for herself. It was really a little more space than she actually needed considering the sheer size of the main house, but with this particular setup she had her own living room and kitchenette so she would have some privacy when the inn was full.

At some point she would love to hire a live-in innkeeper, someone who would work with her and allow her to have time off and away. That had been the plan when she started and it had really grown on her when she and Colton had gotten serious. The thought of being able to take time off to get away for a vacation and having someone in charge who didn't have to live in her apartment seemed like the perfect solution. They had even talked about converting the attic to a small apartment but she couldn't afford to do it right now. Getting the inn up to code had taken every dime her grandfather had left her. Maybe someday she could make it happen.

Not that she was going to be vacationing or taking time off any time soon.

With a sigh, Susannah sat down on her sofa and looked out the front window. Now Colton was walking around out there and even though she couldn't hear him, she could tell he was irritated and desperately trying to make his point.

As she continued to stare at him through the window, it reminded her of another time not so long ago when she did the same...

If it wasn't one thing, it was another, she thought. At some point, Pops was going to have to deal with the fact that this old house needed more than some minor repairs. Another tree limb had fallen and cracked several of the deck steps. Jake was sending one of the guys from his construction crew over to check it out and she hoped she'd be able to get a few words in before her grandfather did. Maybe if she could gently tell this worker how her grandfather needed to be nudged into doing more than a patch job, she'd have a chance of making some headway.

The sound of a car door slamming had Susannah walking to her bedroom window and peering out.

And her heart actually felt like it skipped a beat.

It had been a long time since the mere sight of a man had her feeling quite like this – it felt foreign and then a little exciting.

Turning to glance at her reflection in the mirror, she frowned. She was a forty-five-year-old woman and when she looked in the mirror she saw...a forty-five-year-old woman.

Well that's depressing.

Normally she wasn't quite so critical of herself. On an average day, she felt fairly young and sassy. But now that she was going downstairs to talk to a man who had her feeling like a giddy teenager, she felt every one of her forty-plus years.

Smoothing a hand over her dirty blonde hair, she looked at her reflection again and sighed. Had she known she was going to feel like this, she would have put a little more effort into how she was dressed and maybe put on a little makeup, but it was too late for that now. With nothing left to do, Susannah left her room and went down the stairs and out onto the front porch.

There was no sign of her grandfather and for that she was relieved. When the man from Coleman Construction turned around, she raised her hand to wave, smiled, and...yeah, her heart fluttered again.

He was tall with dark hair that was grey at the temples and when he smiled back she could see he had dimples. Her feet felt like they were glued to the spot and she couldn't move. Not that it mattered. He sauntered over and Susannah swore his eyes never left hers.

Even though he was wearing sunglasses.

"Hey," he said softly, with a bit of a Southern drawl. He held out his hand to her. "I'm Colton Hale. I'm here to take a look at the back deck."

Susannah reached out and shook his hand and had to stifle a moan of pleasure. His hand was large and warm, his skin rough.

And it felt better than it should have.

Swallowing hard, she hoped she didn't look foolish. "Hi, Colton. I'm Susannah Westbrook – Ezekiel's granddaughter. We've been expecting you."

He took off his sunglasses as he stepped up onto the porch. She noticed he had sky blue eyes and she definitely had to force herself not to stare. Colton Hale was everything she found attractive in a man – tall, rugged, and exceedingly polite.

Something she found very endearing as they walked through the house discussing the problem with the deck. They had barely made it out the back door when her grandfather approached them.

"Ah, Colton!" Ezekiel said with a smile. "I was hoping you were the one Jake was going to send. Come on, let me show you the damage we've got!"

Colton looked at her with a lopsided grin. "It was nice meeting you, Susannah. I hope we get to see each other again." And this time when he shook her hand, his touch lingered.

And just like that, she found herself hoping for the same thing.

And that was how it all began.

It started with him coming over for that one repair, but

then it was only two weeks later that Hurricane Amelia hit and the work on the house began. For as much as she had wanted to renovate the big family home for years, it still saddened her how it ended up finally happening. She did her best to preserve the family history and stay true to the design of the house, but she also had fun with decorating it.

And Colton had been there for every step of it.

They were probably the only two people who had been here every single day and seen the entire transformation. She used to tease him how the house was as much his as it was hers simply because of the time and attention he put into it. And here he was still putting in time and attention even when she was certain it was the last place he wanted to be.

She wasn't a fool. She had seen the wariness on his face when he climbed from the truck earlier. So many things were on the tip of her tongue to say to him – to apologize, to explain herself – but she pushed it all aside and opted to stick to business because it was safer. Her ex used to tell her how she always tried to make everything about herself and it was something she was very aware of. The last thing she wanted was for Colton to feel that way about her so maybe it was better to simply *not* talk about herself and her feelings.

But it was slowly killing her.

Unable to take her eyes off of him, she watched as he came back around to the front of the house. He paced the driveway as he continued to talk on the phone. She knew how knowledgeable he was about everything that had to do with construction and on this particular job and she had no doubt he was making his point for why everything that was done was done to code.

She almost felt bad for the person on the other end of the line.

Almost.

In the blink of an eye he was sliding his phone back into its clip on his belt and walking back toward the front porch.

Susannah jumped to her feet and met him in the foyer. "Well?" she asked nervously. "How did it go?" It killed her to see how uncomfortable he looked and she knew it was only partly because of whatever transpired on the phone.

"Well, we need to put a couple of reinforcements on the deck, which isn't a big deal."

"O-kay..."

"But I made him take a look at all the reports and permits on the driveway and the fact that this is a historical property and as such, there are certain codes that are grand-fathered in." He shrugged. "We came to an agreement that it's fine and nothing needs to be done to it."

"Really?" she cried excitedly.

He nodded. "Yup."

"So...that's it? It's all taken care of already?"

Nodding, Colton replied, "Yup. We had all the permits done correctly and if we modify the deck with some extra bracing and do some strategic solar lights, you'll be fine."

"Wow, I...I don't even know what to say. That seemed...I mean...I thought..."

"Yeah, it was a little anticlimactic," he agreed with a low laugh. They stood in companionable silence for several minutes before he took a step back. "Uh, I'm going to head to the building supply place down in Wilmington and get what we need. I should be back after lunch and I'll get it all done before the sun goes down."

"Colt, I...thank you," she said quietly.

"You don't have to thank me, Susannah. We've said

often enough that I'm just as invested in the inn as you are. There was no way I was going to let someone walk in here and hold up your grand opening on some minor technicality."

There were so many things she wanted to say but...she didn't. "Okay then. I guess I'll just...see you later."

With a curt nod, he turned and walked out the door.

If anyone were to ask him, Colton would say he felt good right now. There had been a problem and he handled it without losing his cool and without groveling for Susannah to take him back.

That was progress in his book.

There was still the rest of the day to get through and he knew that meant spending all that time with her once he got back to the inn. She had a habit of watching him work and asking all kinds of questions and he had no idea how he would handle it if she did that today. Maybe she was okay with the way things were between them, but he still wasn't.

And as he pulled back into the driveway a few hours later, he still didn't know what to expect.

Rather than go to the front door and walk through the house, he opted to walk around the outside and set up his tools and ladders under the deck. He had everything just about set up when he heard footsteps over his head. Part of him wanted to howl to be left alone, but there was part of him that was still a little desperate for the sight of her.

She came down the steps and found him securing a ladder against the house. He purposely did it so he could keep his back to her for a little bit longer while he got his emotions under control.

"Hey," she said as she came closer. "Did you have time to stop for lunch? I could make you something to eat."

"Uh...thanks but...I grabbed a burger on my way back."

"Oh."

Colton moved around her and began putting the bit on the drill and loading his tool belt with all the screws he was going to need.

"So, how many of those brackets do you need to put on?"

"Eight."

"And how long do you think it will take?"

He knew what she was doing – it had always been their thing and normally he didn't mind talking to her while he worked.

Just not today.

"Hopefully just an hour or two. But there's a box with the new solar lights in them near the bottom of the stairs if you'd like to take them and line the paths a bit. I bought six for the base of the deck stairs and then a dozen to go along toward the gazebo and another dozen leading to the pier."

"I'm not sure I'd know..."

"You just take them from the box and push them in the ground. No other tools are necessary. After that, the sun will charge them and tonight you'll see how well they work." He turned his back to her again and began to climb the ladder, hoping she'd get the hint and let him be.

She did.

Two hours later – as he had predicted – he was done. Susannah was still milling about in the yard, pondering the perfect placement for the solar lights and Colton allowed himself a minute to simply observe. Even from across the yard he could see the way she was biting her lip as she stuck one of the lights in the ground. Then she stood up and inspected her work while trying to push her long bangs from her eyes.

He knew her every mood, her every pose, every movement – had memorized them over the last year. And even as he watched her now, he could almost hear her second-guessing her decision on where she placed the lights and wondering if she should have let him do them instead. She had done that so many times over the course of the renovation. Susannah had incredible taste and a strong work ethic, yet she lacked the confidence in herself. No matter how many times he praised her or complimented her, she always found it hard to believe him.

And believe in herself.

If he stood here much longer, his thoughts were going to take him places he didn't want to go. He had gotten the work done, took pictures of everything and sent them to the city inspector to show it was all done and scheduled the inspection for the following day. Next he packed up all his tools and supplies and began carrying them out to his truck. Once that was done, he had no choice but to seek Susannah out and let her know he was finished.

Walking around to the back of the house again, Colton noticed she was no longer outside. Climbing the deck stairs, he went to the kitchen door and knocked. It felt ridiculous considering he had full run of the place just a few days ago, but he didn't want to overstep his bounds.

Her smile was warm and welcoming as she opened the door. "You didn't need to knock," she said softly, stepping aside for him to come in. "Are you all finished?"

He nodded and explained that he'd be back with the inspector in the morning.

"And you think everything will pass? There won't be any other issues?"

"I'm going to be here with him so if anything comes up, I'll handle it. There shouldn't have been any issues as it is, so if this guy is going to be a ball-buster, I'm going to be one right back."

She smiled at his words. "Can I get you something to drink? Some water? Sweet tea? Or..."

"I'm good, but thanks. I need to go check on the guys over at the yacht club job. I left them with a list of instructions, but..."

"It's after four, Colt. I'm sure they're gone by now. You always end your day at 3:30."

Damn. She was right.

"Yeah, but...I need to go make sure it all got done and check in with Jake about some inventory issues," he said, not looking at her. He was studying his boots and wishing he could just leave.

"This is crazy," she said after a minute, her voice laced with frustration. "We need to be able to spend time together without you trying to run out the door, Colton!"

"I'm not trying..."

"Yes, you are!" she cried. "I don't want things to be awkward between us! We've spent far too much time together working toward the same thing and I hate that you don't seem to want to be here with me to see it all through."

He studied her hard for a moment. "So that's all this is? About the inn?"

"Um..."

"What is it you want from me, Susannah?" he asked wearily, his hands dropping to his sides helplessly. He didn't want to argue with her, but he certainly didn't want to just be her buddy or the contractor who helped with the inn.

"I just want to talk to you, Colton. I miss talking to you." The sad look on her face told him she was just as miserable as he was. He wanted to tell her she wasn't being fair, wanting to have her cake and eat it too. Unfortunately, this was all new to him and he had no idea what the rules were.

"We've been talking all day and...and I just think it's best if I go."

She took a step toward him. "You know what I meant. We spent all day talking about the inn and the work you were doing. I want a chance to sit and talk about you. Us." She paused. "How are you doing?"

He went from feeling sad to incredulous. Was she serious right now? "How am I *doing*?" he asked with a hint of sarcasm. Over the last year he had never shied away from expressing his feelings in front of her. He knew he was capable of being angry, but never once had he directed that emotion at her.

Until now.

"Um..."

"I'm miserable, Susannah!" he said loudly. "You turned my whole life upside down Saturday night and I'm still reeling from it! How do you think I'm feeling?" He hated seeing her flinch, but she needed to understand just how hurt he was.

If he was expecting her to shy away from a confrontation – like she had on Saturday night when she opted to leave rather than stay and talk things out, he was wrong.

"I'm miserable too, you know! Do you think this is easy for me?"

He saw the tears well up in her eyes, heard the catch in her voice and it was almost more than he could bear.

"I honestly don't know what to think," he said miserably, raking a hand through his hair. "You just walked out Saturday night, Susannah. You didn't want to talk and now you do. Well...maybe I'm not ready to talk yet."

The first tear fell and he saw the defeat in her eyes before she looked away. "I'm sorry. You're right. I...I was being selfish." Then he heard her murmur something under her breath like "When will I ever learn" and how she was being selfish, and he reached out and gently forced her to turn around and look at him.

"What is going on?" he asked softly, his hands gently clasping her shoulders. "You are the least selfish person I have ever met, Susannah, and it pains me to hear you say that about yourself."

"How can you even say that?" she asked as her tears fell in earnest. "I walked away from you – from us – Saturday without taking your feelings into consideration. I didn't want to talk so I didn't. I wanted to leave, and I did. That's selfish, Colton."

Okay, she totally had a point there, but he wasn't going to outwardly agree with her.

"So talk to me now," he coaxed, reaching up to wipe away her tears.

"You said you didn't want to."

He shrugged. "I changed my mind." Unable to help himself, he leaned forward and rested his forehead against hers. "Talk to me, Suz. Please."

Shaking her head, she looked down. "I never wanted to hurt you. You have to know that. And if I could, I would change the way I acted Saturday night."

For a minute, he had hope. Was she saying what he thought she was saying?

"I should have stayed and talked to you," she went on. "And I definitely would have explained to you much sooner why I never want to get married again."

And just like that, all hope was gone.

Again.

Swallowing hard, Colton forced himself to speak. "Tell me why."

But before she could answer, he took a step back and gently took one of her hands in his and led her out to the living room so they could sit. As much as he wanted to hold her while she talked, he thought it was best to sit at the opposite end of the sofa.

For more than an hour Susannah talked about her failed first marriage – most of the information wasn't new to him – but the insecurities her ex inflicted on her were. It was something they had never really talked about. They had each shared a bit about their failed marriages but...Colton looked at Susannah and saw a woman who was a survivor. She had dealt with the end of a bad marriage and stayed strong for her children. He saw her as a success. To hear her talking about the doubts that still plagued her all these years later was a bit of a shock.

How had he missed the signs?

When she finished talking, he could see she was exhausted. Moving closer, he took one of her hands in his. "Susannah, I know I can't sit here and tell you that the way you feel is wrong. No one has that right. But I can sit here and tell you that the woman you just described is not the woman I see."

She blinked at him as if she didn't understand.

"I hate that Mark did all of that to you," he said. "I truly am. But you know what? He's the loser in this scenario. He's the selfish one. Not you. He missed out on so much because of his selfishness." He squeezed her hand. "I may not have ever had kids of my own, but even I know that parenting is hard. And rather than stick around and deal with that, he left. You stayed." He kissed her hand.

"Colton..."

"You stuck it out," he went on. "You had twins to raise and you did it alone. You got them through all the tough years – puberty, high school, dating..." He shuddered for dramatic effect. "And you did it on your own."

"They were my babies..."

"Weren't there days you wanted to just throw in the towel? Days when they made you crazy and challenged every word you said?"

She laughed softly. "They still do. And yes."

"But you stayed. That's not something a selfish person does, Susannah. You raised two amazing people and when Mallory walks down the aisle with Jake, you're going to be there to see it. Mark won't."

She nodded and wiped a stray tear away.

"And when Sam does the same with Shelby, Mark won't be there to see it. When you hold your first grand-child in your arms and see the look on your child's face at the realization that they're a parent now too, Mark won't be there for that either. Why? Because he selfishly walked away from his family because he didn't want the responsibility. And people like that, Susannah, they have to make everyone else look bad so it takes the attention off of their own bad behavior. You weren't a bad wife or a bad person. Mark just needed you to feel that way so he could justify his shitty actions."

"I don't know how to undo any of this," she said after several minutes. "I'm not sure I can."

"You don't have to work all that out today," he said, bringing her hand to his lips again and kissing it. "You take all the time you need."

"But...what about you?"

Good question.

Maybe he was setting himself up for more heartbreak.

Maybe things were never going to work out the way that he wanted. But for Susannah, he'd let her break his heart over and over again if it meant that she came to realize her worth – that she deserved love and to be happy.

Squeezing her hand, he replied, "I'm not going anywhere. We'll get through this together." Then he paused. "That is, if you still want me."

Her smile was both sad and lovely at the same time. Reaching out, she cupped his face in her hands and kissed him.

—

5

The sun was shining.

The batch of muffins were picture-perfect.

And she was happily singing along with Def Leppard about pouring some sugar.

"So...you're back together with Colton."

Susannah jumped as she looked over her shoulder at her daughter the next morning. With a smile, she asked, "What are you talking about?" Walking across the room, she turned the music down.

"Mom, please. I saw his truck here yesterday afternoon and it didn't leave until this morning. I even asked Lisa to open the shop for me because I was waiting for Colton to leave so I could come over and talk to you."

She felt herself blush. "Oh."

"And on top of that, I seem to remember how you usually blasted eighties metal whenever Colton left in the morning – particularly after a date night."

"Oh."

"Oh? That's all you can say? Oh?"

She couldn't help but laugh. "Fine, we'll talk. But why don't you go make us some fresh coffee and heat up a couple of muffins while I finish ironing these cloth napkins. Deal?"

Mallory smiled brightly. "Deal."

Once she was out of the room, Susannah sagged with relief. She was still coming to grips with the last twenty-four hours herself and had been looking forward to having some time to herself when her daughter had shown up.

What she had meant to be a sweet, thank you kiss after Colton said he wasn't going anywhere turned into a wild, sex-fueled afternoon and evening.

And morning.

Just the thought of it still made her blush.

The first few times she and Colton made love back when they were newly dating, Susannah insisted on having all the lights off. She wasn't a young woman anymore and had more than her fair share of body issues. There were stretch marks from having babies and things were a lot softer and saggier than they once were. More than once she had cried at the unfairness of finding a man who made her feel desirable while her own body image held her back.

She got over that eventually and, considering how they made love in the full light of day, she knew Colton had no issues with her body.

And she knew how much she loved his.

He was in incredible shape – largely due to the physicality of his job – and she had spent more than an acceptable amount of time marveling at him. Any time she mentioned how sexy she thought he was, he teased her and said it's because he was still a young guy and she'd have to remind him that he wasn't *that* much younger than her.

Which was another thing that took her a while to get used to.

"I have issues," she muttered, folding another cloth napkin. Ironing was one of her least favorite chores, but this morning it seemed like the perfect mindless task while she had some quiet time.

"Do you want blueberry or banana nut?" Mallory called out from the kitchen.

So much for the quiet.

"Blueberry, please!"

Turning off the iron, Susannah stepped away from the board, walked over to the front window and looked out. Colton left an hour ago and he was going to be back within the hour with the inspector. The last thing she wanted was to have to make small talk with the man who almost caused her to miss her opening date, but she'd do it if she had to.

"So?" Mallory sang as she walked into the room with a tray full of their coffee and muffins. She placed it on the coffee table and sat down with a knowing grin on her face. "Let's talk!"

"You're getting yourself all excited for nothing," Susannah chided as she sat down.

"Oh, really? So you're telling me that Colton didn't spend all day yesterday and all night here last night?"

"I didn't say that…"

"Then are you going to try to say that it was just time for the two of you to talk things out and that's all you did? And that it took all night?"

"I didn't say that either," she replied primly, reaching for her coffee.

"Mom!" Mallory cried with exasperation. "For the love of it! Just spill it!"

A slow grin spread across Susannah's face behind her coffee cup. Sitting up straight, she turned to her daughter. "Would you prefer it if I told you we had a night of wild, monkey sex to some Guns N' Roses' *Welcome to the Jungle* as a way to seal the deal?"

Beside her, Mallory choked on her muffin to the point that Susannah had to pat her on the back to make sure she was all right. "Jeez, Mom! What the hell?"

Still smiling, Susannah took another sip of her coffee. "You were being a little too smug so I figured I'd give you something to think about."

"Ugh...I do not want to think about you having crazy monkey sex. That's just wrong."

"And yet, it happened."

"*Mom!*"

"What?" she cried, laughing. "Are you telling me that you and Jake never had..."

"Do *not* say that phrase again!" Mallory interrupted. "And I'm not saying that we do or don't, but if we do, I'm certainly not going to tell you about it!"

"Oh, stop. It wasn't like I was offering specifics," Susannah said mildly. "I'm just confirming that we did more than talk yesterday."

"Okay, then. Well...good. And other than all the...you know...what's going on with the two of you?"

"It wasn't the easiest conversation to have," she began. "I don't like having to admit to all my flaws."

"You don't have any, Mom."

"We all have them," she corrected. "And honestly, Mal, I carry a lot of baggage because of your father."

"I know and I get it, but...it was so long ago and you're so much better than him and better off without him! We all are! Why are you still letting him live in your head?"

Good question.

"Some things you don't get over too easily."

"I get that, but you're holding on to something that doesn't even make sense anymore. You've proven over and over again that you are this amazing person!" Mallory said, taking one of Susannah's hands in hers. "You are this incredible role model – someone I can only dream of being! You're strong and loving and compassionate and Sam and I are so lucky to have you!"

"Mal..."

"I'm serious! Don't let Dad keep doing this to you. He's not worth it. It's like you keep letting him talk to you even though none of us have heard from him in years! We're all so much better off without him, Mom. Especially you. Don't let what he did ruin what you have with Colton."

Clearly Susannah was the only one who believed the things Mark said to her. But how...

Shifting to get more comfortable, Susannah placed her mug back down on the table and looked over at Mallory. "Do you think we can talk right now as...friends...rather than mother and daughter?"

"Of course," Mallory replied, breaking off a piece of her muffin.

"When you're young and in love, you have confidence and hope and even if you're insecure about something, it doesn't feel so big – and if it does, you tend to get over it quickly."

Mallory nodded.

"You get older and mature a bit and you take what you've learned from all of your previous relationships and they make you into the person that you are. Sometimes it's good, sometimes...not so good."

Another nod.

"I can remember dating your father back in high

school." And for some reason, she smiled. "We were both so young and clueless about so many things, but we didn't care. We found out we were pregnant and even though we were scared, we just felt like we were going to be okay because we had each other."

"I can't even imagine being so young and starting a family," Mallory said before taking a sip of her coffee. "And to have twins must have freaked you out."

They'd had that particular conversation before and it wasn't where Susannah was going with this one.

"Unplanned pregnancy aside, I remember being confident in who I was and how I looked. All during my pregnancy, I still felt good. Your father never commented on my changing body and when it took some time to get back in shape after you and Sam were born, well...I still felt good. I was nineteen and things sort of bounced back, if you know what I mean."

Laughing softly, Mallory nodded.

"But time goes on and your body changes and then your relationship changes and the things you're insecure about get thrown back at you," Susannah explained quietly. "And you don't realize how much damage has been done until it's all you're left with."

"Mom..."

"Colton was married before," she went on. "He was married for ten years until he and his wife just drifted apart. There were no harsh words, no arguing, just two people who simply didn't want to be married anymore. The first time he told me that, I couldn't even comprehend what that was like. I had no idea what to say."

"Everyone's circumstances are different."

"And yet they still shape us. Colton walked away from

his divorce not completely unscathed. In theory, it sounds simple, but he is a man who deserves to be loved whole-heartedly and completely."

"So do you, Mom," Mallory interjected. "Just like you're not judging Colt because the person he was married to before stopped loving him, no one's judging you because of Dad...you know."

She chuckled softly. "I still don't know if I believe that."

"You know, we've never really talked about it – how Dad's leaving affected you."

"At the end of the day, Mal, he's still your father. For better or for worse. I didn't want to be the kind of mother who talked badly about my children's father to them. I didn't want to be the reason you and Sam didn't have a relationship with him – didn't want that responsibility. It was my job to love you both and encourage you on the decisions you needed to make where your father was concerned."

"You know you had every right to trash talk him."

She laughed again. "Yeah, I know. I was friends with several women who were also divorced and they all bitched a lot about their exes and all I could remember thinking was how bitter and petty they sounded. Sometimes they talked like that in front of their kids and I saw how it affected them. I didn't want to do that to you and Sam."

"We always appreciated it. Although..."

"Although...?"

"I can't speak for Sam, but I hate how you couldn't really let your feelings show because of us."

"I didn't look at it that way." She paused. "At the time, it worked."

"I guess. But I think it's also why it took you so long to start dating. You had a lot of emotions to deal with."

"That was only part of it. The real reason I didn't start dating until you were older was because you and Sam needed me more than I needed to go out on a date. My main role in life was being your mother and it's a role I have always loved. I didn't see not dating as a bad thing."

"What made you decide to go on that first date?" Mallory asked. "And I'm not talking about Colton. I'm talking about when we were living back up in New York."

"Oh, my goodness. It was right after you and Sam left for college. My friend Heather asked if I would go on a double date with her. I was terrified. It had been ten years since I'd been out anywhere with a man and over twenty years since I'd gone out on a date with someone new!" She laughed at the memory.

"And how was it?"

"Awkward," Susannah replied, still laughing. "I was so nervous and the guy – I can't even remember his name – but he was such a jerk. He made it abundantly clear that he was looking for someone younger and flirted with the waitress most of the night. Heather apologized profusely and promised to make it up to me. She set me up a few more times before I finally asked her to stop and tried figuring it all out on my own."

"You never talked about it much – your dates and all."

Shrugging, Susannah reached for her coffee. "There wasn't much to talk about. No one really interested me and I never got intimate with any of them. It just felt wrong."

"Wow. So then when you and Colton..."

"Yup." She gave a curt nod. "It had been a long, long time."

"Again, wow."

"Tell me about it."

"Was it...?"

"Weird? Terrifying?" she prompted with a giggle. "Yes. It was all that and more."

Mallory laughed with her. "I'm sure Colton made it all right."

"He was beyond patient with me. I refused to turn the lights on for a long time. I couldn't imagine any man wanting to see me naked. Hell, I didn't even want to see me naked!"

"You're in great shape, Mom, please. You don't give yourself enough credit."

"While I'm dressed, sure, I look good. But take all this off and there isn't anything particularly firm or perky anymore."

Rolling her eyes, Mallory took another bite of her muffin. "That's just part of life."

"Easy for you to say. You're only twenty-seven."

"You know I spent a lot of my teenage years being chubby. I worked hard to get in shape and then to get rid of the freshman fifteen I put on in college."

Susannah patted her daughter's hand delicately. "Someday you'll understand exactly what I'm talking about."

Putting the rest of her muffin down, Mallory faced her. "Let me ask you something."

"O-kay..."

"Has Colton ever said anything negative about your body?"

"Uh...no."

"Does he insist on keeping the lights off?"

She chuckled softly. "Definitely not."

"And he clearly still enjoys sex with you, right?"

If the last twenty-four hours were anything to go by...

Susannah nodded.

"Then what are you so worried about? Do you know how many women your age would *love* to have a man look at them the way Colton looks at you?"

"Um..."

"Plenty!" she cried. "Hell, I see couples come into my shop all the time and most of them look like they barely tolerate each other."

"Well, if they've been married a long time..."

"It has nothing to do with how long they've been married," Mallory argued. "It's about how you *feel* about each other. I've seen elderly couples come in and you can tell just by looking at them how they are still deeply in love. Sometimes they look just as sweet and doe-eyed for each other as a couple in a new relationship! It's precious!"

"I'm not sure what that has to do with..."

"Look, I can't force you to change your mind about marrying Colton. I wish I could, but I can't." Pausing, she let out a long breath. "But I can encourage you to embrace who you are and where your life is at right now."

Tears sprang to Susannah's eyes.

"You're a rock star, Mom. You are this kick-ass woman who came through some really hard times and decided to take on all of this!" She motioned around the room. "You're starting a business and doing something incredible! You never let anyone stop you – not even Dad. You just keep going and watching you and all you've accomplished is inspiring!"

Okay, now she was seriously crying. Reaching out, she pulled Mallory into her embrace. "Thank you."

"I meant every word of it," Mallory said, hugging her tight. "You're the best role model a girl could ever want." Then she pulled back. "And this – what we did just now – I like knowing that we're not just mother and daughter, but that we're friends. So...thank you."

Susannah always had a close relationship with both of her children, but this moment with Mallory was special. She thought of her conversation with Georgia the other day and how she mentioned not having a close relationship with her daughters and right now, her heart truly hurt for her. It bothered her to know that Georgia had no idea how wonderful it was to sit and have a cup of coffee with someone you not only gave life to but who had become one of your best friends. It was something Susannah hoped every mother got to experience.

Hopefully someday Mallory will experience that for herself.

After a few minutes, they separated and finished their coffee and muffins. "So what's up next for the inn?" Mallory asked. "Soft opening this weekend. Are you ready for it?"

"Oh my goodness, I think so!" she said with a smile. "This is a chance to give it a test run before we officially open. We'll open the doors to the public to come in and tour the house and the grounds Friday afternoon and welcome our first official guests. I can't believe it's finally here!"

"You've wanted this for so long. I know Pops would be proud."

"I'd like to think so. You know he hated making changes to this place."

"And yet he left you the money to do just that," Mallory replied. "I don't think he was against having the work done. I think he hated knowing he couldn't help with it. You know he was never good about taking a backseat when there was work to be done."

"Isn't that the truth," she said with a laugh. "Still...

there's a part of me that really wished he could see it – to see that I didn't tear it all apart."

"You know Aunt Georgia would have done that if she got the house."

They both laughed. "No, Georgia wouldn't have torn anything down, but she would have made this place like a museum – someplace you didn't feel welcome or weren't able to sit down and relax."

"Maybe." She paused. "What you created here is just... it's perfect."

"Coming from you, that's a high compliment. I know you love this house as much as I do – if not more."

"Well, I did have a hand in the renovations..." Mallory said with a satisfied grin. "And I happen to think I did a damn fine job with finding the perfect furniture and accessories for you to use."

"That you did." Standing, Susannah looked around the living room and smiled. "It's everything I hoped it would be and it will be the perfect location for your wedding." Mallory stood and began collecting their mugs and napkins. "Which reminds me..."

"Yeah, yeah, yeah...a date. I know. Now that I waited so darn long, I hate the thought of taking a weekend away from paying guests."

They walked into the kitchen. "After this weekend, I'm going to start taking reservations so just tell me which one you want blocked out so I can have the website updated."

Placing the mugs in the sink, Mallory turned and studied her.

"What? What's that look for?"

"What look?"

Her daughter had that look on her face like she had a

secret of some sort. "Come on, Mal. Out with it. What are you thinking right now?"

"Just that you're amazing."

Susannah rolled her eyes.

"I'm serious! We've dragged our feet on setting a date and here you are on the verge of opening this incredible business and you're not giving me any grief about horning in and taking a weekend away from paying guests." She shrugged. "You are completely within your rights to tell me to wait and take my chances."

"If you don't know by now that you and your brother come first with me no matter what, then I don't know what to tell you." She smiled as she said the words and she meant every one of them. "But all kidding aside, have the two of you even talked about a general timeframe?"

"I've wanted to marry Jake for more years than you can imagine..."

Susannah nodded because it was never a secret that Mallory had a crush on Jake Summerford from the time she was a young teen.

"And when he proposed all I could think was how all of my dreams were coming true and I couldn't wait to be his wife."

"But...?" She wasn't sure where this was going.

"I always wanted a wedding here in this house and for it to be big and wonderful! For us to be surrounded by everyone we knew and have it be this massive party."

"And now?"

Mallory shrugged again. "Now I just want to be Jake's wife. I don't care about it being a big party or how many people are there. I'm just ready to start the next phase of our lives."

Unable to help herself, Susannah walked over and

hugged her daughter. "Say the word and we'll make that happen. Heck, it's the holidays. Everyone will be in town already and the place will be decorated for Christmas..."

"A Christmas wedding would be amazing!"

"Just think of all the evergreens and twinkly lights...the giant Christmas tree in the front window would make the perfect backdrop for vows..."

Pulling back, Mallory looked around. "Oh, my goodness! That's tomorrow, right? We're meeting the crew here to decorate tomorrow afternoon at three?"

"Yup. And it's going to be beautiful!"

"We're cutting it a little close, aren't we?"

"I wanted everything to be fresh for the public tours. I didn't want to take a chance that anything would wilt or brown. And I certainly don't want artificial trees." Together they walked back to the grand foyer. "Georgia's going to come and help too."

"Mom..." Mallory whined.

"She has impeccable taste and a real flair for decorating for the holidays. She knows she's not in charge, but I figured we could always use an extra pair of hands."

"Maybe."

The sound of a car door slamming had them both looking toward the front door. "That's Colton with the inspector," she said nervously, swallowing hard. "I really hope everything passes and we can move on. There's so much to do! And now you're thinking of getting married at Christmas and..."

Mallory took both of Susannah's hands in hers. "Breathe, Mom. Just breathe. The last thing I want to do is stress you out. I still have to talk to Jake about all of this so... let's just put this on the backburner for right now and focus on the opening this weekend, okay?"

She nodded and walked over to the front door, pulling it open. Colton was standing in the driveway and as he turned to smile at her, her heart fluttered.

Just like it always did when he smiled at her.

And as he began to walk toward her, she felt confident that everything was going to be all right.

6

OPENING DAY WAS A SUCCESS. The response to the tours
of the inn and its grounds were met with nothing but praise
and Susannah found herself getting more than a little
emotional. How she wished her grandfather could see how
magnificent the old house looked and the wonder on her
guests' faces when she talked about the history of both the
property and the town. Every word she spoke, every fact she
shared, every story she told, she learned from him. Pops had
such pride in this home and this town that sharing it seemed
like a fitting tribute. And as much as he hated the thought of
seeing the family home change, she had a feeling he still
would be proud.

Strong arms gently wrapped around her waist and she
let out a soft sigh as she leaned against Colton.

"The inn's a big hit," he said softly, resting his cheek
against hers. "Not that I expected anything less."

She hummed softly, enjoying the feel of his arms
wrapped around her. He had been her rock through this
entire process. He'd helped her make decisions and listened
to her when she needed to talk. There was no way today

would have felt like the success that it was without him standing here beside her. Now they were standing in the small living room in her private quarters staring into the fire and it was the perfect end to a perfect day.

"After hearing nothing but construction noise for so long and then a whole lot of quiet because it was just me here, it was nice to have the house filled with laughter today."

He nodded and kissed her cheek. "You made everyone feel welcome. And I think it was brilliant to offer this weekend preview to members of the press and social media influencers to help spread the word about this place. I'm sure there are going to be nothing but rave reviews coming your way and you'll be booked up for the coming year before you know it."

The thought made her smile. "That would be amazing. But I can't take all the credit for the idea. Mason's fiancée was the one who suggested it after I talked with her a couple of months ago about handling some of the social media marketing."

"Plus, she and Mason got a night here at the inn," he teased.

"Oh, stop," she said, laughing softly. "Family is welcome here any time they want."

"Still, it's better that they get the chance now while they still can."

Pulling away slightly, she turned and looked at him. "You mean because of the baby?"

"No, I mean because there aren't going to be any vacancies for a long time. I'm certain of it."

Reaching up, she caressed his face. "You are very sweet to say that, but I don't want to get too ahead of myself. The grand opening isn't for another couple of weeks. This was really just a test run."

"A successful test run," he confirmed. He hugged her close before stepping away. "I should be going."

Confused, Susannah turned around and faced him. "Going?"

Nodding, Colton picked up his coat from the sofa before smiling at her. "It's late and I shouldn't be here."

Now she was even more confused. Walking closer to him, she asked, "Why shouldn't you be here? Don't you want to see how breakfast goes tomorrow?" The words were spoken lightly but even she could hear how nervous she sounded.

He was standing in front of her and reached up to caress her cheek. "Susannah, it's not proper for me to spend the night here when you have guests. I know we know most of them personally, but it's still not right. I don't want anyone making any snide comments about the innkeeper sleeping with the handyman or anything like that."

She couldn't help but laugh at the image. "Colt, that sounds a little like bad porn right there. No one's going to think anything of it. All the rooms are upstairs. No one will even know you're here."

And that's when she knew exactly what was wrong. Even without considering the sad smile on his face, it even sounded wrong to her own ears.

"Colton, that's not...I mean..."

His hand on her cheek stilled. "I'm not looking to be your secret, Susannah. There was a time when we kept things quiet when Sam was still living here, but that was different."

Reaching up, she held his hand to her. "I don't want you

to go," she said softly, urgently. "I want us to celebrate all we accomplished together."

If it were possible, his smile turned even sadder. "Sweetheart, I'd like nothing more than that, but not at the expense of your reputation."

"I think you're being a little old-fashioned," she teased, hoping to lighten the mood.

But he shook his head. "Nope. I'm just being respectful of you." Then he leaned in and kissed her before wishing her a good night. "Lock up behind me."

She stood there for a solid minute before walking out and locking the front door. And as she walked back to her rooms, Susannah still couldn't believe he left. Not once while they planned the opening or even while they talked about every aspect of the business did she consider what people would think of Colton spending the night. She had a right to a life, didn't she? And his sleeping over wasn't anyone's business but her own!

Locking the doors to her apartment, she considered calling him and demanding he come back but thought better of it. Still, the whole situation didn't sit right with her and once everyone was fed and settled in the morning, she was going to do something about it.

It was late and Colton knew he should be asleep and yet he couldn't seem to make himself close his eyes. Lying in his bed alone, he stared up at the ceiling and forced himself to think long and hard about the state of his life.

Leaving Susannah's earlier was the right choice, even though he hated it. In a perfect world he wouldn't have to be coming home alone because he and Susannah would be living in the same house.

And married.

Yeah, he still was having to come to grips with that one.

He wasn't lying when he said he wasn't going anywhere earlier in the week. He knew he'd rather be with her than without her. But was he fooling himself?

For as long as he could remember, Colton wanted to be married. Hell, he'd wanted to be married and have a family. His parents had always had a good marriage and it was because of them that he believed it was possible. Not that they were perfect, but he watched them work together to overcome struggles and hard times. He heard them fight but he also saw them make up. He could remember hearing them both apologize to each other. And as he grew up, that was the image he had of what a marriage should be – two imperfect people who forgave each other when mistakes were made. Two people who were in it together.

By the time he and Dana had gotten married, he discovered that it wasn't quite like that. Hell, he had even contemplated not getting married because what they had wasn't the same as what his parents had. It wasn't until he voiced his concerns to his mother that she sat him down and explained some hard truths to him.

"Every day in a marriage requires work," she said. "Some days you'll barely like each other and that's okay. But what you have to understand – what you have to accept – is that no two people can agree on everything all the time. There's compromise and there's accepting that there are going to be things you'll never agree on."

"I get that," he replied. "But...there are times when I don't feel like there's the connection between me and Dana like you have with Dad."

She laughed softly and hugged him. "Oh, Colton, no two couples are the same. And your father and I aren't like most couples we know. We remember to take the time to laugh together every day and not take everything so seriously. It takes an effort sometimes but it really is important not to go to bed angry. Sometimes you have to let go of the petty stuff or bite your tongue or let the other person have the last word. In the long run, it's worth it." She paused. "Not that I'm saying one of you has to be a doormat..."

"I know."

"Don't compare you and Dana to anyone else. You'll end up being disappointed. Be who you're meant to be together and everything will be all right."

But everything wasn't all right.

When his marriage failed, he had to come to grips with the fact that his dream died a slow, painless death. He felt like a complete failure and had been embarrassed to tell his parents they were getting divorced. And, in typical fashion, they didn't judge; they simply told him they were there for him if he needed them.

Boy, did he need them now.

They'd both been gone for a while – his mother passed away eight years ago, his father, five, and he missed them both terribly. What he wouldn't give to talk to them right now and get some wisdom from them. He knew they would encourage him to follow his heart, but he was so afraid to trust it. He understood that marriages failed all the time, but he couldn't understand how his could have failed considering how badly he wanted it to work.

And then he met Susannah.

By that point in his life, he had accepted the fact that he'd never have children of his own, but he had hope in getting a second chance at marriage.

"Why?" he whispered into the darkness. Colton held no illusions about himself. He wasn't the greatest looking guy and he certainly wasn't rich, but he was a good man – a caring man – and a hard worker. He didn't drink, didn't do anything illicit; he was just an honest, average Joe. Didn't that count for anything? He wasn't asking for much – hell, he was just asking for a woman to love who loved him in return.

And for that woman to want to marry him.

Although he and Susannah hadn't talked about that particular aspect of their relationship, he wasn't sure if the desire to be married again was going to just go away for him. He knew that it was entirely possible that one morning he'd wake up and decide that simply being her boyfriend wasn't enough.

So where did that leave him and where did he go from here?

Of course, now wasn't the time to bring it up with Susannah – certainly not now; it was practically the middle of the night. But also not in the next several weeks or months. She had enough on her plate with the holidays, the inn opening, and the possibility of Mallory and Jake finally getting married. He wanted to be respectful of her time and her feelings, but he had to remind himself that he had feelings too that deserved to be respected. If they were going to move forward, he had to remember that this wasn't a relationship for one. He loved Susannah and would do anything for her, but he had needs as well.

"This is getting me nowhere," he murmured.

Rolling onto his side, he punched his pillow a few times and tried to get comfortable. He hated sleeping alone. Granted, there were plenty of nights when he and

Susannah weren't together, but if he had the choice, he'd prefer to have her sleeping beside him.

And it wasn't just about the sex. At his age, he knew he was a little beyond his prime, but now he appreciated things he didn't when he was younger – like the intimacy of simply holding someone while you lay in the dark and talked. Or curling up together in your sleep because your subconscious knows how much you love the contact. There was something very comforting about lying in bed together at night and talking about your day and listening to them talk about theirs. There were many nights when they didn't talk at all but just read side by side – him with a good crime novel and Susannah with her romances. It was comfortable and while to some it would seem boring, Colton knew he wasn't looking for the excitement of his youth, he wanted a partner to share a life with.

Yawning, he closed his eyes and tried to clear his mind. Tomorrow was another day and all he could do right now was to take things a single day at a time.

Maybe what they had was enough.

Maybe he didn't need to get married again – after all, what if Susannah got bored with him the same way Dana had? He wasn't sure he'd survive that twice – not only because he was the common denominator in both those situations, but because his feelings for Susannah were so much more than he had ever felt for his first wife.

And that's when it hit him – maybe that was already what was going on and why Susannah didn't want to marry him. Maybe she was sparing his feelings and saying the issue was with her, but really, his boring ways were already a factor.

Flipping onto his back again, he let out a long breath and cursed. There was no way he was going to get any sleep at this rate and rather than fighting it, he kicked the blankets off and climbed from the bed. In nothing but his boxers, Colton strode out to his kitchen and poured himself a glass of water and took it out to the living room with him. The silence was the enemy right now and with no other choice, he clicked on the TV and settled in for some channel surfing to distract himself.

It was going to be a long night.

"Do you think people will judge me if Colton sleeps here when there are guests?" Susannah blurted out the next morning when Mallory came over to see how things were going with the guests.

"Um...hey. Good morning to you too," she said with a smile, walking over to the antique buffet table in the dining room and helping herself to a glass of juice. Glass in hand, she turned back to Susannah. "I'm sorry, what was the question again?"

Susannah relayed the conversation she had with Colton the night before and spoke in hushed tones because guests were still coming and going. "So? He's being crazy, right? I mean, no one's going to think anything of it. He's just being overly cautious."

"Well..."

"No," Susannah interrupted. "People aren't that closed-minded about things like this anymore. And besides, it's no one's business! It's not like I've got a revolving door of men sleeping with me! It's one man and one that I love! Doesn't that count for anything?" It wasn't until she noticed Mallory's eyes had gone wide and then heard someone clear their throat that she realized just how loud she had gotten. Luckily, when she turned around, she saw it was her nephew Mason and his fiancée Scarlett. Embarrassed, Susannah scurried around wiping down a table for them, offering them coffee and juice.

Mason kissed her on the cheek before doing the same to Mallory. It wasn't until he had Scarlett seated that he spoke. "So, um...not that I was eavesdropping..."

"Oh, God..." Susannah groaned.

"But if I could add my two cents to the topic," he said with an easy grin.

"Mason," Mallory interjected. "Maybe you shouldn't."

He held up a hand to stop her. "Look, personally, I agree with you. It isn't anyone's business who you're involved with and whether or not they're sleeping here with you."

"Thank you."

"However," he continued, "you know what small town life is like. Now, granted, you aren't only opening your doors to the people of Magnolia Sound to stay here, but your guests are going to be interacting with the people and business owners in town and...well...you know, people talk."

"But they've been dating for a year," Scarlett commented. "I don't see what's different all of a sudden."

"Thank you, Scarlett," Susannah said with a smile, pouring her a glass of orange juice. "Nothing's different."

"Except now people are staying here and you've opened the home to the public and – therefore – to scrutiny and gossip too," Mallory said. When Susannah tried to comment, she stopped her. "Look, I'm not saying I agree with it, Mom, but it's just something you need to be aware of. When you own a business in this town, everyone feels like they have a right to comment on what you do and how you do it. I get it at the shop all the time. People come in and will comment on what pieces of furniture they don't like all the way to whether or not they like what I'm wearing that day! And don't even get me started on when they come in and comment on something Jake or Coleman Construction did! It's maddening!"

"I had no idea..."

Scarlett nodded and raised her hand a bit. "Now that Mallory's mentioned it, I can totally agree. I saw it with my dad's garage and my grandfather's bar. People talk. And it's not always about the business itself. You get one uptight guest in here or someone local suddenly gets wind of or actually sees Colton's truck here all night and it will become part of the dialogue when people talk about the inn."

"I can't believe that would happen," Susannah scoffed.

"But are you willing to take that chance?" Mallory asked. "Look, as a mature and responsible adult, one could argue that this is your house and you can do what you want."

"Exactly!"

"However," Mallory went on, "it could also be argued that you're old enough to handle not sleeping with your boyfriend every night. So if he isn't here on the nights you have guests, it shouldn't be a big deal."

"But what if she's booked every night for months?" Mason asked. "She and Colton aren't allowed to...you know...during all that time?"

Both Scarlett and Mallory laughed but Susannah wasn't amused.

"Look," he said, "I'm not saying you two can't get busy on your own while the guests are out or maybe you have someone working overnight so you can go to his place, but that's going to get old fast."

"Ew, you did *not* just talk about my mom getting busy," Mallory said with disgust. "That's just gross."

"Oh, grow up," he said with a laugh, pouring himself a cup of coffee. "We all do it and personally, I think it's great that she and Colton have a good sex life!"

"No one said that!" Mallory cried.

"If they didn't, then we wouldn't be talking about finding a way for Colton to spend the night," he countered. "If she wasn't interested in sex with him, then she wouldn't care about sending him home at the end of the day."

"Okay, okay, okay," Susannah said quickly. "That's enough. I'm not...this is not the conversation I want to be having and now I'm completely mortified."

"Mom, you don't have to be mortified. Sex is a completely natural part of a healthy relationship. That is what you once told Sam, wasn't it? You know, after he came home and saw Colton leaving?"

Groaning, Susannah hung her head and shook it. Why had she thought it was a good idea to ask her daughter about this?

"Of course, this wouldn't be an issue if you would have accepted Colton's proposal," Mallory added.

"Holy crap! Colton proposed?" Mason asked loudly and Scarlett punched him in the arm. "Sorry. I just...wow! How come you turned him down? We all thought that's where you guys were heading."

Straightening, Susannah looked from Mason to Scarlett to Mallory and then back to Mason. "You did?"

He nodded. "Hell yeah. You guys were great together and it was nice to see you so happy. Plus, Colt's a really cool guy. I always enjoy hanging out and talking with him when the family's all together." Then he paused. "Wait...if you turned him down, why are you worried about him sleeping here?"

"Just because she turned down his proposal doesn't mean she wanted to end things with him," Scarlett said, but Mason was shaking his head.

"Then he's a better man than I am. If I had proposed to you and you turned me down, I don't think I would be able to keep dating you."

Scarlett patted his hand. "Dude, we're having a baby. If I had turned down your proposal, we still would have been involved with each other."

Rolling his eyes, he explained, "That's not what I meant. If circumstances were different and you weren't pregnant and I proposed…"

"Ah, got it." Then she nodded. "Yeah, I don't think I would want to keep dating you if I turned down your proposal."

"What if you just weren't ready?" Susannah asked, fascinated at the turn in the conversation. "I mean, what if you loved him, but you just weren't ready to get married?"

Scarlett considered that for a moment. "Well, I think we would have talked about it and maybe agree that I'd accept the proposal but that we wouldn't even think about planning a wedding until I was ready."

Interesting.

Looking at Mason, Susannah asked, "And how would that have made you feel? Would you prefer putting a ring on her finger even though there's a chance she might never want to get married?"

"Hmm…I don't know. I don't know if I could keep going like that. In the back of my mind I'd always be wondering if she was ever going to change her mind. It would put so much extra pressure on the relationship. Plus, I think I'd start wondering how long I'm supposed to wait. If I'm the kind of guy who wants to get married, that means I want a marriage and kids and all that goes with it. Am I supposed to give up on what I want while I'm waiting for her to figure out what's stopping her? I mean, I'm an awesome catch!"

Scarlett smacked his arm playfully. "Feeling pretty full of yourself this morning, Bishop. What's up with that?"

"Oh, please, I'm like this all the time and you know it," he teased right before leaning in and kissing her.

While they seemed to get lost in each other, Mallory slowly walked over to Susannah. "Seems to me there's a lot more for you to consider than just being able to sleep with your boyfriend."

And as she strolled from the room, Susannah had to agree.

7

"Dinner was delicious as usual, Susannah. Thank you."

She smiled at him as she stood to begin clearing the dishes. Colton joined her, carrying his own plate to the sink. "You know you don't have to do that," she said softly.

With a shrug, he said, "And you know I don't mind helping."

It had been four days since the soft opening of the inn and while he couldn't quite put his finger on it, he could tell that something was on her mind. This was the first time he'd been over since that night – not that he was purposely avoiding her, but he really needed the time to himself to figure out how he truly felt about moving forward without getting married. Plus, now that the inn was finished, his focus was on other Coleman jobs and by the time he was done for the day, he was tired and dirty and it was easier to just go home to his place.

"You're awful quiet tonight," she said after a minute. "Everything all right?"

Here was the perfect intro for him to talk about his feelings.

"Yeah," he said instead. "Everything's fine. Just a little tired. This job over at the yacht club should have been a no-brainer, but we've had inventory issues and I had two guys out sick today and there's rain in the forecast and that's going to set us back on top of the holidays, so..."

She walked over and gently guided him back to his chair and then stood behind him, massaging his shoulders. "I'm sorry. And it's been so cold out too. I hate thinking of you working outside like that."

Her hands felt so good that Colton instantly began to relax. "I'm used to it. I've been doing this for over twenty-years so I barely notice the weather anymore."

"Still," she said, her hands kneading deeper, "I wish you didn't have to work so hard."

It was something she started saying after they began work on the house. Colton had a crew full of guys who were younger than him and as foreman, he probably could get by with delegating what needed to be done. That wasn't the way he worked, though. He was a hands-on guy and that meant if his guys were swinging a hammer, so was he.

Her hand hit a particularly sore muscle and he hissed.

"Sorry," she whispered.

"Nothing to be sorry for. It feels good."

"That wasn't a sound of something feeling good," she teased.

"Trust me." His head leaned back and rested against her which caused him to hum with approval. "How about you, Suz? How was your day?"

"Still going over the comment cards everyone filled out this weekend and trying to make adjustments for the grand opening."

"What does that mean? Did people complain?"

"No. Not really," she said, moving her hands so they were both working his right shoulder. "More like suggestions."

"Such as?"

"There were a few suggestions about the selection of toiletries we offered – some of the scents were not a hit."

"Okay, that's not huge."

"One complaint about the pillow selection…"

He glanced over his shoulder. "Seriously?"

She nodded. "A little like Goldilocks – one was too firm, one was too soft…"

"Good grief."

"Another person wrote that I didn't have enough gluten-free and vegan options for breakfast, but I asked everyone when they made their reservation about dietary needs and restrictions so I'm not too worried about that one."

"You know you're not going to be able to please everyone, right?"

"I know." Now she shifted to his left shoulder. "But in the beginning, I really need to be aware of what people want and try to accommodate as much as possible. So if that means having extra pillows stocked, I'll do it. If I have to add a few items to the menu, it's not a big deal. Same with the toiletries. I'll add a couple of varieties."

"I just don't want you killing yourself and jumping through hoops. That's all."

Leaning down, she kissed him on the cheek. "Don't worry, I won't." Giving his shoulder one last squeeze, she stepped around him and finished putting the dinner dishes in the dishwasher. When she was done, she came back over and sat down beside him. "I'm glad you came over tonight."

Reaching out, she took one of his hands in hers. "I missed you."

Colton couldn't help but smile. "I missed you too, beautiful." He loved seeing her blush when he called her that.

"I baked some apple cobbler for dessert. You know, when you're ready."

She definitely spoiled him. Susannah was a fantastic cook and she seemed to get real pleasure from making special treats for him.

And he appreciated each and every one of them.

Placing a hand on his stomach, he grinned. "I'm still full from the pot roast, but thanks." He paused. "So have you finalized your Christmas plans? Will everyone be here for Christmas Eve or Christmas Day? I know you and Georgia were deep in discussion over that last time we talked about it."

She laughed softly. "Christmas Eve here, Christmas Day at Georgia's. You're coming to both, right?"

"Uh..."

Truth be told, he wanted to. He planned to up until a week and a half ago. Now he wasn't so sure of his place and didn't want to be the guy hanging out where he didn't belong.

As if reading his mind, Susannah sighed. "Colton, we've got to talk about this."

"I don't know what you mean." And honestly, he couldn't be sure what exactly she was referring to. "I don't expect you to invite me to every family gathering, Susannah. I don't need to be with you for both. And besides, your cousin might not appreciate my being there."

"Don't be ridiculous. Georgia loves to entertain and the more the merrier." She smiled at him sadly. "And that's not completely what I was referring to."

He arched a brow at her and waited for her to explain.

She let out a long breath. "I know things got a little... awkward...but you said you weren't going anywhere and... you kind of have."

"Excuse me?" Straightening in his chair, he studied her hard. "What's that supposed to mean?"

"It means...it means you left the night of the opening and you didn't come back until tonight."

"Susannah..."

"No, I know you have other jobs you need to focus on, but I feel like you're pulling away and...and it bothers me."

"You can't have your cake and eat it too," he murmured, raking a hand through his hair as he jumped to his feet.

"Meaning?"

"Meaning, you can't keep pushing me away with one hand and pulling me back with the other!" And yeah, he was frustrated.

"That's not what I'm doing!" she cried.

"Let me ask you something," he began and didn't wait for her to respond. "Do you love me?"

Her expression softened. "You know I do."

"But not enough to marry me," he stated.

"You know why..."

"Honestly, Susannah, I don't. I mean, I know what you've told me – I know what you've been telling yourself, but I think it's a convenient excuse."

"*What?!*" Now she stood and stalked over to him. "How dare you!"

"Sweetheart, you and I both know that you are an extremely levelheaded, confident woman. You don't shy away from a challenge of any kind. You're an amazing mother who raised two incredible kids! You tackled turning this old house into a bed and breakfast that is going to be a huge success! Everything you put your mind to, you give it your all and make it succeed!"

"You don't know..."

Reaching out, he grasped her shoulders. "Yes, I do! And do you know how I know that?"

She shook her head.

"Because you're an extremely intelligent woman who worked out every possible angle for this business and put it into play! Because people love you and you make them feel welcome! Because you made this place the kind of destination where people are going to want to stay!"

"Colton..."

"You've taken a chance on so many things, Suz. Why not on me?" And damn, he hated how desperate he sounded, how needy, but he couldn't help it. He needed to know.

Her mouth moved but no words came out and he cursed himself for backing her into a corner like this.

Then he cursed again and claimed her lips with his.

It wasn't tender or sweet, but a little untamed. Her arms wrapped around him just as his went around her – as if they both needed to be as close as humanly possible. Her soft curves always drove him wild. He loved being able to grab and caress them and he loved the sounds Susannah made when he did.

Without breaking the kiss, he lifted her onto the counter and stepped between the vee of her legs and growled with how good it felt. He might not be a young man anymore, but he still enjoyed making love – especially with Susannah. They'd come a long way since those early days when she wouldn't let him even look at her naked.

Speaking of...

His hands snaked under her t-shirt as he pulled back

long enough to whip it over her head. Diving in for another kiss, her legs wrapped around him. It didn't seem possible that they could still feel this kind of urgency for each other. Ten minutes ago, he was exhausted and couldn't imagine anything feeling better than the shoulder massage she was giving him. But now he was wide awake and wanted her. Needed her.

Reaching up, he cupped her breasts, the calluses on his hands snagging on the delicate lace covering her. He used to feel bad about it, but he knew from experience how much she loved how rough and scratchy his skin was.

The kiss went on and on – changing, softening, before going deep and wet again. In a perfect world, he'd strip them both down right here, right now. But the back kitchen wall was floor to ceiling windows along with a pair of French doors leading out to the deck. Mallory and Jake were known to walk through that door without any advanced notice and the last thing he wanted was for Susannah to be caught in a compromising position.

They'd had that happen more than once while Sam was still living here and he wasn't looking forward to it ever happening again.

Susannah's nails scratched along his back before trailing up his neck and into his hair.

He loved when she did that.

It still amazed him that she was this wildly attracted to him. He knew he was still in decent shape because he had such a physical job, but he also knew his hair was graying, he wasn't quite as firm in places that he used to be, and...his stamina wasn't what it once was. He'd lost count of how many times he had silently wished he and Susannah had met when he was younger and more in his prime.

Judging by the sounds she was making and the way she

was rubbing against him, she didn't have a problem with any of it. And that's what spurred him on to lift her back off the counter and stride out of the kitchen to her suite of rooms. No one was staying at the inn tonight and that meant he wasn't going anywhere.

Still, he kicked the door closed just in case anyone stopped by unannounced.

He didn't stop until they were in her bedroom and he was gently placing her on the bed where they finally broke the kiss. Both were more than a little breathless but the way she looked up at him was beyond sexy. He pulled his shirt up and over his head, tossing it aside before he reached out and let his hand skim up her belly to her breasts again.

"You're beautiful," he whispered. "I could look at you all day."

Even in the dim lighting of the room, he could see her blush. "Stop," she said quietly. "You don't have to say that."

"I know I don't have to, but I want to because it's true."

"Colton..."

He placed a finger over her lips. "Shh. To me, you are the most beautiful woman in the world." He swallowed hard. "Always have been. Always will be."

A soft smile crossed her face. "I love you."

"I love you too," he said gruffly, lying down beside her. He touched her – gently skimming his hands along her arms, her face, her throat. There was no rush to finish stripping them down, no need to hurry. They had all night.

Even though he had to be up at five a.m. to go to work.

Still, a night of slowly making love to Susannah was worth missing out on some sleep.

They rolled toward each other as they began to kiss again – her lips soft and a little wet against his. Her skin felt warm and wonderful and for several moments, they simply enjoyed the pleasure of this lazy exploration. It was familiar. It was comfortable. Some nights it was all fast and frantic, but tonight felt a little more intimate.

And he was more than okay with that.

Lazily, he stripped off her jeans and panties and she helped him remove his pants and boxers. There was one small bedside lamp on and he had to admit, he loved looking at her. She had such soft skin that was fairer than his and he loved the look of his tanned hands touching her. Her back arched beneath him as he caressed and teased her. Her breath caught when his mouth latched on to her nipple. And she cried out his name over and over as he made love to her.

And later, as they lay together in a tangle of limbs, she placed a soft, sleepy kiss on his chest. He could tell she was practically asleep and he hugged her a little closer.

"Stay," she whispered. "Always stay."

A smile tugged at his lips as he reached over and turned out the lamp. Kissing the top of her head, he replied, "Okay."

All day the next day, Susannah had a smile on her face. She felt good. Happy.

Almost deliriously so.

And with George Michael singing on the 80s station she had on, she allowed herself to sing and dance just like she had back in high school.

It was four in the afternoon and Colton said he was coming for dinner again. Well, she had invited him for dinner before he left for work this morning and he accepted. She had a chicken roasting in the oven and had just put a salad together that she placed in the refrigerator. As she moved around wiping down the granite countertops, she couldn't help but let her mind wander to the night before.

Having Colton work on the Inn meant he was here with her almost every day for a year. She got used to seeing him every day – looked forward to seeing him. Once the work was done and he had to move on to other jobs, they still saw each other every day. Sometimes they'd meet up in town for lunch, but they tended to eat dinner together every night and took turns staying at each other's homes.

This new turn in their relationship really forced her to think about what she wanted for them and their future.

Mallory had oversimplified things the other day when she said it was just about sleeping together.

But it wasn't.

The truth was, she wanted to go to sleep beside Colton every night after they talked and laughed and shared a meal together. She wanted to wake up in the morning and talk about what they each had planned for the day. It would be a lie for her to say sex wasn't a factor. It was. But really, it was more of a bonus because even if they never had sex again, she enjoyed the companionship they shared. He made her feel good about herself and Susannah hoped she did the same for him. And even though they could keep things as they currently were, she wanted to live with him and if that meant taking the big, scary leap and getting married again, she'd do it.

Was she scared? Yes. Was she suddenly over all her insecurities? No. But at the end of the day, she knew Colton accepted her for who she was – the good and the bad, the insecure and the confident. Why hadn't she realized that sooner?

Feeling like a weight had been lifted from her shoulders,

she decided that she'd broach the subject with him tonight. Although...how was she supposed to come out and ask him to propose again? Was that even allowed? Proper?

With a groan, she considered calling Mallory and getting her input but the sound of footsteps coming through the front door stopped her. She glanced at the clock and wondered if it was Colton arriving already. Was she ready for him? For this? For all that she wanted to say?

She held her breath as she waited for him and when he turned the corner and strode into the kitchen, she couldn't help but feel giddy.

This was it.

She was ready.

He smiled as he stepped in close and pulled her into his embrace, kissing her softly, thoroughly.

When Colton lifted his head, his eyes scanned her face. "All day," he said gruffly. "I looked forward to this all damn day."

She melted against him, her arms wrapping around his waist. "Me too."

Resting his head on hers, she could almost feel him smile. "Really?"

She nodded. "As a matter of fact, I was just thinking about you and how I couldn't wait to see you." Taking a steadying breath, she led him across the kitchen and asked him to sit down. "Can I get you something to drink? A snack?"

He chuckled softly. "I'm good. Although I wouldn't mind a shower. I thought I'd go home first and do that, but I just couldn't wait to see you."

That single comment boosted her confidence.

She sat down beside him and reached for one of his hands. "So...I wanted to talk to you." His expression fell slightly and she was quick to reassure him. "It's nothing bad, I swear! At least...I don't think it's bad."

"O-kay..."

For a minute, Susannah tried to work out what she wanted to say and the right way to say it.

"Susannah?"

She let out another long breath and stared at their joined hands. "Okay, here it is...I thought I was doing the right thing when you...you know. I was a little shocked and surprised by your proposal and I let fear make my decision for me."

Looking up at him, she saw his expression was fierce but he didn't say a word.

"I've done nothing but regret it," she went on. "Every minute of every day. I've thought long and hard about everything – about what I want out of life, about us..."

"And?" he interrupted, his voice barely a whisper.

Shifting in her seat, Susannah took a moment to collect her thoughts. "You have to understand. I thought I was doing the right thing."

"You said that already."

"I know, I know. This is much harder than I thought it would be." When he went to interrupt, she stopped him. "You deserve to have someone without so much baggage. Someone who will be a good wife for you. Someone who's good enough."

His grip tightened on her hand and he tugged to get her attention. "You listen to me, Susannah Westbrook. I am done listening to you talk about yourself like that! Don't you get it? Don't you understand by now? There is nothing wrong with you! Any man would be lucky to have you!"

"But..."

"No!" he snapped. "So what if you weren't enough for him – for Mark? You're more than enough for me!"

Tears stung her eyes. "Colton..."

He shook his head again. "No, everything you're saying – all of your fears – that was a long time ago. That was before. You can't let the words of a man who walked away from the amazing family he had rule your thoughts, Susannah. He doesn't even deserve consideration in anything you do or say because he was wrong. So very wrong. You are everything that is good and sweet and pure in this world!" Reaching up, he cupped her face. "I am honored that you think so highly of me – that you think I deserve so much. But all I want – all I *need* – is you. Don't you get that?"

She nodded as the first tears began to fall. "I do. I really do," her voice cracked as she spoke. "And maybe I'm too late...and it's okay if I am...I just..." She looked up at him. "I want to be with you. Forever. Whether it's as your wife or your girlfriend...I don't care. But I want us to live together and...and..."

She never got to finish. Colton hauled her into his lap and claimed her lips with his and kissed her until they were both breathless. When he lifted his head, he smiled at her. He shifted them around until Susannah was seated in the chair while he stood.

And then he got down on one knee.

"Oh my goodness! What is happening?"

Reaching into his pocket, he pulled out his wallet and then...the ring.

Her ring.

Holding it up to her, he said, "I wasn't sure I'd ever get a second chance at this with you, but I was hopeful." With a lopsided grin, he placed the ring on her finger. "I love you and nothing would make me happier than you agreeing to be my wife. My forever."

"There is nothing I want more in this world!" she said, leaning forward and wrapping her arms around him. "If I could, I'd marry you right now. Tonight!"

He held her tight. "I'd love nothing more than to make that happen. But first, I'm going to kiss you again."

And he did.

And he kept on kissing her until Susannah was ready to drop to the floor with him. Instead, she pulled back and smiled. "How about we go inside and celebrate?" Standing, she held out her hand to him until he was on his feet in front of her.

"That sounds perfect."

They hadn't gone more than a few feet when there was a knock at the back door. Turning, they found Jake and Mallory walking in – both of them grinning from ear to ear.

"Mal?" Susannah asked. "Everything okay?"

"New Year's Eve!" she said excitedly. "We're going to get married on New Year's Eve!"

"I DON'T WANT to say your daughter stole our thunder, but..."

"Yeah, she totally stole our thunder," Susannah agreed. It was just after nine and they were in bed after finally getting some time alone to celebrate.

After Mallory's exclamation, they had opened a bottle of champagne to toast the good news. It took almost an hour – and scrambling to add enough side dishes to include her and Jake for dinner – before Mallory noticed the ring on Susannah's finger.

"Oh my goodness! Is this...? Does this mean...?"

More champagne was poured and another round of congratulations spoken before they got back to the topic of a New Year's Eve wedding.

And another hour before they finally left.

"You sure you're up for putting a wedding together on such short notice?" Colton asked, breaking into her reverie.

She shrugged and snuggled up beside him. "It was kind of my suggestion," she admitted. "When Mallory mentioned to me a couple of weeks ago how she wished they had gotten married already and that she hadn't procrastinated for so long, I suggested the holidays since everyone is going to be in town – including Jake's parents."

"I know they both said tonight how they didn't want anything big..."

"I have to admit, I'm a little envious of them."

He smiled and placed a soft kiss on the top of her head. "Really?"

"Yup. They're not going to agonize for months or years over details that, in the grand scheme of things, really don't matter. They just want to be married in a simple ceremony, surrounded by family and friends. And I think that sounds perfect."

"You do, huh?"

She nodded.

"So for us..."

Tilting her head back, she grinned up at him. "I want exactly the same thing. Small. Intimate. And here. This is where we first met and this is where we spend so much of our time. Working on this house brought us together so it seems only fitting that we should get married here."

He chuckled softly.

"What? What's so funny?"

"A few days ago you were so against getting married that you were damn near having a fit and now you're making plans for us and...I like it."

"Just like?"

He kissed her again. "Actually, I love it. And yeah, getting married here at the inn would be the perfect spot for us. You just tell me when and I'm there."

"If Mallory hadn't claimed New Year's, I would have suggested it." She sighed. "It would have been perfect. I guess now we'll have to wait a little while so we don't…you know…"

"Steal their thunder?" he finished with a hint of amusement.

"Yeah, something like that." She sighed again. "This is what I get for not being smart enough to accept your proposal the first time. I'm so sorry."

"Susannah, you have nothing to apologize for. No one could have predicted things turning out like this. And besides, we can still plan and maybe even move in together before we actually get married. That is, if that's something you'd consider."

"I would. I definitely would. It just would have been nice to…"

"I know," he said quietly, his hand gently rubbing up and down her back. "It's not the way I would have preferred it, but…I think we've already established that this is where we want to be. And, if it's that much of a deterrent to us, maybe we just go down to the courthouse and get married and have a ceremony with friends and family later."

She perked up a little. "That could totally work! We could go to the courthouse and then take the time to plan out the perfect time to celebrate. Ooh…maybe Valentine's Day!" She paused. "Or is that too clichéd?"

"Even if it were, it wouldn't matter to me. Any day that you say you want to marry me, I'm there." He yawned loudly. "But we don't have to decide that tonight, do we?"

"Well…"

"Because it was a long work day and then all the celebrating and the champagne and making love and…"

Placing a kiss on his chest, she laughed softly. "You're tired. I know. Me too." Colton reached over and turned out the bedside light. "I love you."

"Love you too, beautiful. Thank you for wanting to be my wife."

"Thank you for wanting to ask me again."

And before she knew it, they were both asleep.

"Okay, guys! Let's break for lunch and we'll tackle standing this temporary wall up when we get back," Colton said to his crew the next day. They all agreed and turned to leave. His phone vibrated in his pocket and he saw he had a couple of texts from Jake asking him to come to the office. There were no reasons listed, just a request for him to come in and that Jake was providing lunch.

With a shrug, he walked out to his truck and began to make his way across town.

It had been a good day so far – the job was back on track, the inventory issue had been straightened out, and if the weather cooperated, they'd be at the perfect stopping point by the time the holidays hit. Maybe that's what Jake wanted to talk to him about. Or maybe he wanted to talk about whatever job Colton would be taking on next. Whatever it was, he wasn't worried. He and Jake had worked together for years and they had never had an issue where a job was concerned and he doubted that would start to happen now.

Although, they were going to be family soon. Was that going to make things weird? Awkward? He hoped not. Lord knew he wasn't ever going to ask for special treatment. The only thing he was going to ask for was time off when he and Susannah got married so he could take her on a honeymoon. They hadn't talked about where they wanted to go, but if it were up to him, he'd take her someplace tropical where they could spend the day lying in the sun. He remembered her talking about how she'd never taken a real vacation before. Anytime she had time off from work, she had come to Magnolia Sound to visit her grandfather and family. Well... now he could take her someplace and let her experience doing something for herself.

Just the thought of it made him smile.

He pulled up to the Coleman Construction office and parked. Inside, he went straight to Jake's office and found his door open. He knocked, just to be polite. "Hey, Jake."

Looking up, Jake smiled at him. "Hey, Colt. Come on in."

So he did.

"I grabbed us a couple of sandwiches from the deli along with some chips and drinks. Why don't you have a seat?" There was a small conference table in the corner of the room that Jake motioned to and once they were both seated, he spoke. "I wanted to apologize for yesterday."

His sandwich was halfway to his mouth when he froze. "Um...what?"

"Yeah, when Mallory and I barged in on you and Susannah. We should have called first. To be fair, we had no idea you had just...you know...proposed. And then we went and announced our date without even asking about yours."

Colton was about to speak when there was a knock on the door. Turning, he saw Sam walking in. "Sorry I'm late. Old Mrs. Mills was a little chatty and I couldn't get a word in edgewise!" he said with a laugh. He sat down at the table and thanked Jake for the food before grinning at Colton. "Hey, Colt! I hear congratulations are in order!"

Seriously, he felt himself blushing. "Uh...yeah."

"I knew Mom would come to her senses. She just needed to get out of her own damn head."

Colton merely nodded. He figured that was the safest response.

"I was just talking to Colt about how I felt bad that Mal and I interrupted things right after he proposed last night," Jake explained.

Sam laughed again. "My sister always has the worst timing."

"Hey!" Jake said, but there was no heat behind his words.

"Oh, stop. I'm her twin so I'm allowed to say things like that." He took a bite of his sandwich. "So I hear that the wedding – yours and Mallory's," he clarified, "will be on New Year's Eve, right?"

Jake nodded.

"Any idea when you and Mom are going to make it official?"

Colton felt a little awkward talking about this without Susannah here, but he figured there wasn't anything wrong with it. "We're probably going to go to the courthouse sooner rather than later so we don't take away from Jake and Mallory's big day and then have a party at a later date."

Both men looked at him like he was crazy.

"What? What did I say?"

"Why would you do that?" Sam asked. "Why go through the hassle of doing both?"

"Honestly? We don't want to wait. We both want to move in together but we're a little old-fashioned and want to be married first."

"What does that have to do with going to the court-house? Why not have a ceremony with all of us?"

He sighed. "I just explained that. We don't want to take away..."

"Yeah, yeah, yeah," Sam interrupted. "I get that, but

Mom's entitled to and deserves something more than going to a damn courthouse."

"I agree, Sam," Colton said. "I really do. But with the holiday's and Mallory's wedding..."

"Shit," Jake murmured, tossing his sandwich down. "You guys wanted a holiday wedding, didn't you?"

"We hadn't gotten that far by the time the two of you showed up. It wasn't until later on that we talked about it and wished we could have done it sooner rather than later."

"Well damn," Sam said around another mouthful of sandwich. "I get that you guys want to do things right by getting married before moving in together, but...and I'm not trying to be disrespectful or anything...but you guys have been spending...you know...your nights together for a long time. You're practically living together already. I just think you should move your stuff over to the big house and plan a ceremony where we can all be there to witness it and celebrate on the same day. Please. Talk to my mother about this or I will."

"Sam..."

"What? Are you seriously telling me you're okay with doing things this way, Colt?"

"I'm just so damn happy your mother accepted my proposal that I'm willing to do whatever it takes to make her happy. We already went and got the marriage license this morning so we can just go and do it whenever we want. And if doing the courthouse thing does that..."

"Okay, everyone just...calm down," Jake said. "Maybe we all need to sit down together."

Before anyone else could speak, Sam started laughing – softly at first and then a little more heartily.

Colton and Jake looked at each other before looking at Sam. "What is so funny?"

"Look at us!" Sam cried before laughing again. "We are three grown-ass men sitting here trying to make wedding plans! Are you not seeing how funny that is?"

"Um...no..." Colt said.

"Not really," Jake added.

"Trust me, it's hysterical and it's almost more than I can handle."

"Look, time's not on our side right now," Jake said. "Christmas is less than two weeks away and then New Year's is right behind it. We're all busy and it's going to be hard planning one wedding. How the hell are we supposed to plan two?"

"That's what I'm saying," Sam explained. "You're not planning two. Mom and Colt can still move in together and plan something for after the holidays and after yours and Mal's wedding. It's not ideal but under these circumstances, I think it's the only option to keep everyone sane."

As much as he hated to admit it, Sam's plan made sense.

He just hoped that Susannah saw it that way.

"I'll talk to Susannah after work and see how she feels about it. But if it makes her uncomfortable, then I'm not going to push," he said firmly. "You guys can come to the courthouse with us and we'll go out to dinner or something and it will be fine. All I want is for your mother to be happy."

He was about to say more when his phone vibrated. Taking a quick bite of his sandwich, he pulled out his phone and saw there was a lumber delivery that had arrived early. Muttering a curse, he stood and took another bite of his lunch.

"Everything okay?" Jake asked.

"Delivery showed up early and if I don't get there in the next ten minutes, they're leaving." With a small growl of frustration, he packed up his lunch and scooped it up. "I hate to eat and run and all, but..."

"No worries, Colt. We can talk later. It's not a big deal. Go."

"Thanks."

Waving to them both, he walked out the office door and was about to head out into the hallway when his drink nearly slid out of his hands. He got himself situated a bit better and was about to walk away again when he heard Sam say, "Dude, I have the perfect solution to all of this. You're going to think I'm crazy but...trust me. It's gonna be amazing!"

His curiosity was piqued, but he had to go.

Muttering a curse, he strode down the hall and made a mental note to call Jake later on and see what this perfect solution was.

"So I was thinking that we can add more twinkly lights to the yard and rent another half-dozen of those heat lamps and put them out on the deck so we can have the ceremony outside and then come inside afterwards for dinner and dessert! What do you think?"

Susannah was listening patiently as Mallory mapped out exactly what she wanted for her wedding and as much as she was impressed at how much her daughter had thought everything through, there was a part of her that was a wee bit jealous at how perfect it all sounded and how much she wished she had thought of it first for her and Colton.

"Mom?"

"Oh, sorry, sweetheart. I was just trying to envision it all in my head."

"And? Doesn't it sound perfect?" Mallory asked excitedly. "And with all the Christmas decorations still up it's going to be so beautiful!"

Nodding, Susannah agreed.

"And the absolute best part – I think – is how we can all go outside at midnight and watch the fireworks on the Sound! It will be the perfect ending to a perfect day!"

Another nod. "As long as the weather cooperates."

"Mom, why would you even say that?! The weather has to cooperate. It just *has* to!"

Standing, she patted Mallory's hand. "I'll see what I can do." Walking over to the refrigerator, she poured them each a glass of sweet tea before sitting back down. "Have you thought about your dress?"

"I have. I actually saw it in town at Vintage Violets," she explained before taking a sip of her tea. "It was in the window last week and I walked by and thought...that's it! That's my dress!"

"Wow! Did you buy it already?"

"That's kind of why I'm here," she said slowly. "I was hoping you'd come into town with me to see it. I haven't even tried it on yet but I called and asked Vi to put it aside for me."

"Mal, I'd love to!"

"Yay! Then you can look for a dress too!"

"Oh, um...Colton and I haven't..."

"I mean, the mother of the bride needs to look fabulous and I'm sure you'll find something amazing there."

Swallowing hard, she smiled and nodded. "Right. Mother of the bride dress."

Mallory's expression turned thoughtful. "Were you

already thinking about a wedding dress for you? Because I'm sure we can shop for that while we're there."

"Um..."

Jumping to her feet, Mallory reached for her hand and tugged. "This is going to be so much fun! I can't even remember the last time we went shopping for dresses together! C'mon! Let's go! I'll call Jake and tell him I won't be home for dinner. You call Colt and tell him the same. We'll shop and then go grab a bite to eat somewhere."

"Mal, I don't think we'll be gone that long. It's barely three o'clock!"

Rolling her eyes, she tugged on Susannah's hand again. "It's definitely been too long since we've gone shopping together if you think this is going to be quick. We're having a girls' afternoon and evening. No arguments. Now go call Colton and I'll call Jake and we'll meet in the foyer in ten minutes."

"How long do you think it's going to take to make a call?"

With a sweet smile, Mallory replied, "The call should only take two minutes, but you're in yoga pants and a t-shirt. You need to get changed and freshen up. Deal?"

Looking down at herself, she realized her daughter had a point. Standing up, she sighed dramatically. "Okay, fine. I'll go change."

"Wear your khaki capris and the coral V-neck t-shirt. That looks really good on you."

"Don't you think it's a little cool outside for that?"

"Oh, right. Okay, keep the capris but pair them with those cute boots you bought at the end of last season and the cream-colored cable knit sweater. That looks good on you too and you'll be warm enough that you won't need to carry a coat with you."

Seriously, her daughter had a great eye for fashion and thought way more about it than Susannah ever did. "Fine. Ten minutes."

Nodding, Mallory walked out of the room and Susannah saw her go into the library to make her call. With a little pep in her step, she went to her rooms and quickly changed and freshened up her makeup before calling Colton. It went directly to voicemail and she hated to back out on dinner plans with him, but...it was just going to be burgers on the grill for them and she hoped he wouldn't mind her making them tomorrow.

"Hey, you reached Colton Hale of Coleman Construction. Leave a message after the beep and I'll get back to you. Thanks and have a good day."

Smiling because she loved the sound of his voice, she waited for the beep and said, "Hey, wonderful man. Don't hate me but...Mallory came over and asked me to go dress shopping with her. She thinks she found her wedding dress and really wants me to see it. Then she wants us to go to dinner, so...I'll have to take a raincheck on our barbecue tonight. I hope you're having a good day and I'll text you when I'm heading home. If you're up for it, maybe you can come over and we can watch *The Tonight Show* together. Love you. Bye."

She hoped he would be up for coming over later. Although, depending on how late she and Mallory were out, she wouldn't blame him if he opted to stay at his place tonight. Maybe Mallory could drop her off at his house or maybe...

"Mom! C'mon! Let's go!"

Sheesh, was it ten minutes already? Glancing at her bedside clock, she saw it was and knew how impatient her daughter could be when she had something she wanted to do. Grabbing her purse, she turned on one of the small bedroom lamps before walking out of the room. "Ready!" she called out as she walked out to the foyer.

"I knew that outfit would look good on you!" Hooking her arm through Susannah's, Mallory hugged her close. "Thank you for doing this with me. I'm so nervous!"

Laughing softly, Susannah led her out the door, locking it behind her. "What on earth are you nervous about?"

"What if the dress doesn't fit? What if it looks horrible on me? What if..."

"Mal, if it doesn't fit or it looks bad, then we'll look for something else. It's not like this is the only dress in town."

"And what if we don't find anything for you? I mean, we don't have a lot of time and with the holidays coming up, the mall will be a nightmare!"

"Plus, the nearest mall is an hour away. That's something that would require a day trip, don't you think?"

They climbed into Susannah's car and Mallory chattered on about how they could potentially be done at Vintage Violet's quickly and still get to the mall if they needed to.

Susannah silently prayed they wouldn't have to and spent the remainder of the drive listening to Mallory run through every shopping scenario under the sun while wondering what she had gotten herself into.

9

"Are you ready for me to start carving?"

Susannah looked over her shoulder at Colton and smiled thankfully. "Yes, and thank you. I thought I was organized but I feel like I'm all thumbs today."

It was Christmas Eve and it seemed like it popped up out of nowhere. All the gifts had been purchased, wrapped, and placed under the tree. Plus, she finished all the grocery shopping and had even managed to prep most of the food in advance. All she had to do was cook and yet it felt a little more overwhelming than usual.

Kissing her cheek, Colton stepped around her and washed his hands. "I would think things would have been a little easier this year. With Georgia and Beau backing out at the last minute, that means a lot less people here for dinner."

Yes, her cousin and her family had asked if she would mind them skipping dinner with everyone tonight. They felt like they needed a quiet Christmas Eve with just Georgia, Beau, Parker, Peyton, Mason, and Scarlett. Susannah didn't mind. After the long talk she and Georgia had a few weeks ago about the state of her marriage, it was probably a good thing that they were trying to reconnect as a family. They were all going to get together tomorrow for dinner at their house so...

"Suz?"

"I shopped and prepped for dinner for fifteen and now we're half that," she said, sprinkling the top of the green bean casserole with french fried onions. "And Sam and Shelby are leaving early to go have dessert with Shelby's parents and then they're going to midnight mass with them at the church."

Beside her, Colton chuckled.

"What's so funny?"

He shook his head and tried to stop laughing, but it took him a minute. "Don't you think it's funny how rebellious your son used to be and now he's marrying the preacher's daughter and going to church on Christmas Eve?"

Okay, that had her laughing a bit too. "Fine, it's a little funny, but it's also incredibly sweet. It's nice seeing him so happy."

"I agree." He paused and studied her.

"What?" she asked nervously. "Is there something on my face?"

Another soft laugh was out before he stepped in close and turned her to face him, wrapping his arms around her waist. "You realize what an incredible job you've done, right?"

She looked at him with confusion.

"You raised two amazing people, Susannah. Your son turned into an incredible, respectful man who is turning heads in this community for all the right reasons."

"I knew he'd get there eventually," she said with a small smile.

"And your daughter is going to be getting married here in this house in a week. You taught her to follow her dreams and she's here doing that and marrying one of the best guys I've ever known."

"They really are perfect for each other..."

"I just thought you needed the reminder of how amazing you are," he said, leaning in and kissing the tip of her nose. "Now let's get this dinner on the table because it all smells amazing."

While Susannah placed the casserole in the oven to brown, Colton carved the turkey. Mallory came in and began taking side dishes out to the dining room along with Shelby. Out in the living room, Jake and Sam poured drinks while talking with Jake's parents about life in Arizona.

Minutes later, when they were all seated around the table, Susannah couldn't help but smile. Her son sat at the head of one end of the table and Colton sat at the other. It felt good – right. And as they all joined hands so Colton could say the blessing, she said an extra prayer of thanks because she was so grateful for all the people here with her.

"Amen," they all said in unison and immediately began serving the food.

Conversation flowed from how work was going for everyone to all the hype for the holidays and funny Christmas shopping stories. There was a lot of laughter and it was loud and boisterous and wonderful. She looked around the table and wondered how soon it would be before there were grandbabies joining them and already knew she couldn't wait for that to happen.

But she'd keep that to herself for now. They had Jake and Mallory's wedding to get through, then hers and Colton's and, hopefully, not long after, Sam and Shelby's.

"Did you hear how many people are going to be at dinner tomorrow?" Sam asked with a smirk.

"I thought just the usual – us plus all the Bishops and then Aunt Grace and the boys. We haven't seen them in a while and I know Georgia tends to conveniently leave them out of family events, but..." She shrugged. "Why? Is there more?"

"According to Mason it's all that and more," Sam explained. "They invited Scarlett's whole family too – her father, her grandfather, her brothers, and her best friend Courtney."

"Courtney's going?" Mallory asked before taking a sip of her wine. "That's new."

Sam took a drink of his own wine. "According to Mason her folks opted to go on vacation for the holidays and Courtney decided to stay home."

"It's going to be very crowded around the dinner table," Susannah mused. "Maybe I should call and offer to host everyone here."

"Mom!" Mallory cried. "You can't possibly put another holiday meal together on such short notice! All the stores are closed!"

Laughing, Susannah shook her head. "Oh, no, sweetheart. I didn't say I'd be cooking. Georgia has that all worked out. I just meant we can have everyone here because there's more room." Pausing, she thought about it. "Do you think I should call her and ask?"

"She may take offense to that," Sam said. "You know how pissy she gets about you and this house."

It was true but...she felt like they had finally turned a corner in their relationship. "I'm going to call her after dinner and just put it out there. If she says no, that's fine. But if she's being hospitable enough to invite so many extra people, then I'm sure she might appreciate a little more space. Depending on the menu, we could even do it as a buffet and spread out a bit. It wouldn't be the first time we celebrated a holiday like that."

"It will be just like our wedding!" Mallory said excitedly. "I love the idea of not sitting down to a formal dinner – no offense, Mom."

"None taken," Susannah replied with a wink. "And the number of people she's having isn't that much less than how many we're having here on New Year's Eve. It could almost be like a test run."

Mallory's smile grew. "I'm kind of loving this. Do you think she'll go for it?"

"I try not to expect anything where Georgia is concerned, but she may surprise us all. I feel like she's mellowing a bit."

"I think we can all thank Scarlett for that," Sam commented. "After all the crap Mason had to deal with, Scarlett confronting Aunt Georgia about it was kind of epic. I wish I could have been a fly on the wall for that."

"We all do," Susannah said with a wink.

Conversation turned to – of course – wedding plans and Susannah loved hearing the excitement in her daughter's voice and then watching the pure joy on Jake's face. They were meant to be together and she couldn't be happier knowing their marriage was going to be a success.

"I still can't believe you found a dress so fast," Shelby said. "That was certainly a stroke of luck that you saw it in the store window like that."

"I know! And it was my size and..." She stopped and sighed happily. "It was just perfect. When I stepped out of the dressing room and saw the look on my mom's face, I knew it was definitely the one."

Everyone looked to Susannah and she nodded. "I was skeptical that anyone could find their perfect wedding dress in the first shop they visited, or that you should buy the first and only dress you try on, but trust me, there was never going to be a more perfect dress for Mallory."

"And the best part was that Mom not only found her mother-of-the-bride dress, but her wedding dress too!"

"Mallory!" Susannah cried, her fork slipping from her hand.

"What? What's the big deal? I think it's amazing you found both dresses!" She looked at Colton and her smile grew. "You are definitely going to be impressed. She looked amazing."

Reaching over, Colton took one of Susannah's hands in his and smiled. "Your mother looks beautiful no matter what she's wearing. She could wear jeans and a sweater to marry me and she'd still be the most beautiful bride in the world."

"Aww..." Everyone said in unison and Susannah felt her cheeks flame with both embarrassment and love for the man sitting beside her.

"And we had so much fun shopping," Mallory went on. "I think we were both a little stunned at how easy it was and so we did our last-minute Christmas shopping too before going and grabbing some dinner. It was the best night."

"You're both so lucky," Shelby said, her smile a little sad. "I don't think I could do something like that with just me and my mom. We'd make each other crazy."

"Well, you don't have to do it alone," Susannah said. "You have me and Mallory to go with you to act as buffers. And we'll make an entire day of it whenever you're ready."

Shelby's face brightened and she looked over at Sam

excitedly. "I think I'm going to like having more women on my side."

Sam grinned and raised his glass. "I'd like to propose a toast – to all the amazing women at this table. I'm thankful for each of you. Cheers!"

"Cheers!"

It was late by the time everyone left and Colton couldn't believe that they were all going to do it again tomorrow. He grew up with a very small family and most holidays were spent with just his parents and grandparents. The few distant relatives they had never came around for Christmas. So this was all kind of new to him, but he found he really enjoyed it. The conversations and the traditions that Susannah had created...well, he could see how much they meant to her and Sam and Mallory.

Staring into the fire in Susannah's suite, he could hear her moving around in the main part of the house, turning off lights and talking to herself. Sometimes he wondered if she even realized she was speaking but figured there was no need to ask. He thought it was adorable and wouldn't want to embarrass her or make her think she had to change.

Letting out a long breath, he slid his hands into his pockets and contemplated a conversation he wanted to have with her about their wedding. After that day in Jake's office when he overheard Sam mentioning that he had a solution, he'd been a little hesitant to admit how he'd overheard the comment. It took him several days to get up the courage to reach out to Jake and ask him about it.

And he had to say, he was pretty damn impressed with what Sam came up with.

But he was afraid to bring it up to Susannah.

Tonight he had pulled Sam aside to talk with him and he was all for Colton deciding when and where he wanted to let Susannah in on the idea, but Colton still hadn't decided. Mallory had joined the conversation and suggested waiting until New Year's Eve to let her mother in on the plan, but he wasn't sure that was the right way to do it either.

"You know what I was thinking?" Susannah asked as she breezed into the room.

"Um...no."

"That when the kids start having kids, they should all stay here on Christmas Eve so we can watch them open gifts! I'll make sure to blackout the dates so we don't have guests and this way we'll always be able to have a family Christmas! What do you think?"

"I think it sounds great in theory..."

"But...?" she prompted.

"But...they might want to have their own traditions now. And when they have kids, they may want to be home on Christmas morning."

"Hmm...I hadn't thought of it like that. Although, I guess we all live close enough together that we could still have breakfast or brunch together. I can't imagine that Shelby's folks would mind. I know there's always a service on Christmas morning so her father would be busy with that. And Jake's folks are always welcome here..."

Walking over, he pulled her into his arms and kissed her on the forehead. "You're getting ahead of yourself here. Let's get through this Christmas and New Year before we start trying to figure out where everyone will be eating breakfast next year."

"I suppose."

"But I do like the idea of blacking out the holidays so there aren't guests here. At least for Christmas Eve and Christmas Day. I know I'd enjoy having it just be us."

Pulling back, she looked up at him and gasped.

"What? What's the matter?"

"In all the time we've talked and planned for the opening of the inn and then with our getting married and you moving in, I never once asked you if you were okay with the house never really being ours! I mean, like we may never be alone in it! There's the potential of people always staying here. Are you...can you handle that?"

The worry on her face and the way there was a slight tremble in her voice told him she was genuinely upset and he did he best to put her mind at ease. "Susannah, I was well aware of what life would be like living here. That's why I'm glad you have this suite of rooms to give us privacy. Even if people are moving around the main part of the house, I know we have our own cozy space right here that no one else can access." He hugged her close again. "So relax. I'm good with it all. As long as I have you, I can deal with anything else life throws our way. Even people sleeping in all the beds upstairs and eating in our dining room."

She visibly relaxed. "What did I ever do to deserve you?"

A slightly snarky comeback was on the tip of his tongue, but then it was Susannah's tongue gently teasing his lips and all thoughts of anything funny – or words in general – went out the window.

He loved the way she kissed and as they went from the slow and lazy kind to ones that went deeper, Colton carefully maneuvered them across the room, down the hall and to her bedroom.

Soon to be *their* bedroom.

As they stood beside the bed, Susannah's hands snaked under his sweater and began moving it up his body. He broke the kiss long enough to pull it off before diving back in to kiss her again. Her hands roamed over his chest and they felt so smooth, so wonderful, he knew he'd never get tired of having her touch him.

She surprised him by abruptly breaking the kiss and taking first one step and then another away from him. He was about to ask if she was okay, but the impish grin on her face told him she had a plan.

And who didn't love a woman with a plan?

Without breaking eye contact with him, Susannah slowly began unbuttoning the hunter green sweater she was wearing. When he spotted a hint of bright red, Colton had to clench his hands at his sides to keep from reaching out and helping her undo the rest of the buttons. He inhaled deeply and almost growled with need when she finally peeled the garment from her shoulders.

"I must have been really good this year," he said gruffly, studying Susannah standing there in her black slacks and red lace bra. Swallowing hard, he took a step toward her and felt relieved that she didn't stop him. One large hand rested on her waist and he saw she was a little breathless – could see her pulse racing.

She'd always been beautiful to him, but her confidence mixed with a hint of vulnerability was possibly the most attractive thing about her.

Slowly licking at her bottom lip, Susannah nodded. "You've been very good." Her voice was a husky, sultry whisper and he was instantly hard.

So many thoughts were running through his brain, but

he had to see what she was going to do next – take off the bra or her pants?

He seriously hoped it was the pants. He was dying to see if the panties matched the bra.

And with a little shimmy, Susannah moved around him and let her slacks fall to the floor. Bending over, she picked them up and – holy hell, she was wearing a thong!

First. Time. Ever.

Tossing the pants onto the chair in the corner of the room, she struck a pose as her smile grew. "So? What do you think?"

I think I forgot how to breathe...

Colton took one step toward her and knew his own smile had to be a bit wolfish. "I think you're a living, breathing fantasy."

She blushed and looked away briefly before meeting his gaze again. "I...I wasn't sure about the thong." Laughing softly, she shook her head. "I'm kind of glad for the dim lighting, God only knows how much cellulite is showing."

She tended to do that – to not fully see just how sexy and desirable she was.

Well...he was about to prove to her that she was.

Closing the distance between them, he dropped to his knees in front of her, raining kisses along her belly to her hip bone. His hands reached around and grabbed her ass and gently squeezed. "I love this," he growled against her skin.

With her hands on his shoulders, Susannah moaned as her head tipped back. "Stop," she whispered. "You don't have to say that. I'm certainly no supermodel."

His mouth continued to kiss and lick and taste her. "No, you're not. You're better." Sliding his hands around, his fingers hooked into the sides of her thong and slowly pulled it down.

"Colton," she panted as she tried to move away from him, but he wouldn't allow it. His mouth found new places – better places – to taste and tease, and within minutes she was writhing against him. His name came out as both a plea and a promise and as she came apart for him, he thought no sound had ever been sweeter.

Kissing his way up her body, he didn't stop until he claimed her mouth – and that kiss was as deep and wet and carnal as they came.

Quickly, he helped her remove her bra before he took a step back to get himself undressed. "On the bed, Susannah," he said and he barely recognized his own voice. His hands shook and it took more than a couple of tries to get his own pants off. When he was as naked as she was, he crawled onto the bed – up her body – and settled in against the softest, warmest skin he'd ever felt.

He was home.

And as Susannah wrapped herself around him and began to move beneath him, Colton knew there was no place in the world he would rather be.

This wasn't quite the way he envisioned things going tonight and he knew there was a conversation they still needed to have, but not tonight.

Tonight his girl had other plans for them and he was more than willing to go along with them.

10

"Okay, I don't want you to panic, but the flowers are wrong."

Mallory was sitting at the antique dressing table in the guest room in Susannah's suite on New Year's Eve and simply smiled at her mother in the mirror. "Wrong flowers or wrong amount?"

That was an odd question...

"Um...they sent two bouquets," Susannah explained. "One is white roses and the other is white lilies."

"Hmm..."

"That's all you can say? Hmm? Mallory, you need to call the florist! There's probably a bride out there tonight missing her bouquet!"

Turning on the upholstered bench, Mallory looked up at her, her smile still in place. "Mom, relax. I'll make the call. It's not a big deal."

Taking a couple of steadying breaths, Susannah tried to calm down. "You're right. It's going to be okay. I don't know why I'm so nervous!"

Standing, Mallory walked over and hugged her. "Probably because your baby girl is getting married in less than two hours."

Hugging her tighter, she felt tears sting her eyes. "Oh, right. That." She took a minute to compose herself before pulling back and cupping her daughter's face in her hands. "How is it possible? It feels like yesterday that I was bringing you and Sam home from the hospital! It doesn't seem right that you're all grown up and getting married tonight!"

"And before you know it, Sam and Shelby will be doing it too. Now that he's proposed, it's only a matter of time."

"Oh, stop. I can't imagine your brother being in a rush to walk down the aisle. I know he says he'd marry Shelby tomorrow, but...I think that's just big talk from him. He can't have mellowed that much."

Moving back to her seat on the bench, Mallory checked her reflection before picking up her makeup brush again. "I think he has. Shelby's been really good for him and person-ally, I love it."

"She's a very sweet girl and I agree, she's perfect for him."

"Isn't it amazing how all three of us not only found our forever loves here in Magnolia, but how within the next few months, we'll all be married to them?"

Just the thought of that was enough to make her smile. Nodding, she said, "Well, we don't know when Sam and Shelby are going to set a date and Colton and I haven't set one either, so..."

Mallory gently placed the brush down again and turned around to face her. "You should do it tonight."

"You mean pick a date?" She shrugged. "I don't know if tonight's the night for that kind of discussion. I mean, we've got a houseful of guests coming and there will be a lot of distractions..."

Standing, Mallory said, "No. I mean...you and Colton should get married tonight. You already have the license and..."

"Mallory, have you lost your mind?" she cried. "I can't... there's no way...Colton would never..."

Stepping forward, she placed her hands on Susannah's shoulders to calm her. "Hear me out, okay?"

Right now, the only thing Susannah could hear was her own heart pounding in her ears. Get married tonight? That was crazy and impulsive and just not possible!

Was it?

"So, a couple of weeks ago, Sam threw out the idea of having a double wedding."

"You mean for you and Jake and him and Shelby, right?"

She shook her head. "No, me and Jake and you and Colt."

It took a minute for that statement to set in. "But...why? Why would he even think of something like that?"

"Honestly? He didn't like the idea of you having a wedding at the courthouse. Neither of us did. You said you were fine with that and Colton said you were fine with it, but...we know you, Mom. I know you were saying it was okay with you because you didn't want to take away from my big day and potentially Sam's."

Her children knew her too well.

"So here's the thing. You deserve something wonderful and romantic and special just like the rest of us – possibly even more than us – and you should have it. Don't settle for something that you don't want when you can have some-thing completely amazing." Reaching down, she took both of Susannah's hands in hers. "Share this day with me. Have a double wedding with us."

Her heart was racing so hard she thought she was going to hyperventilate. "Oh, Mal, I...I can't! I'm not prepared! Colton's not prepared! It would be crazy!"

"You have the dress and all the people you would have invited are already here. There's more than enough food and champagne and cake to cover two happy couples." She squeezed Susannah's hands. "Actually, I ordered a second cake. You know...just in case."

"A second cake? Mallory..."

"Jake and I talked about it and he thinks it would be amazing to have one of his best friends sharing his big day with him." She paused. "And I know having one of my best friends sharing mine would mean the world to me."

Tears rolled down her cheeks and she couldn't believe how selfless – how incredibly generous and gracious – her daughter was being.

"I...I don't even know what to say," she said softly.

"Say yes," a deep voice said from behind them. Turning, she saw Colton standing in the doorway, looking incredibly handsome in his suit. Jake and Mallory had opted for a less formal ceremony and the navy trousers with the burgundy vest he had chosen were perfect.

Mallory quietly excused herself and closed the door behind her. When they were alone, Susannah suddenly felt like a bundle of nerves. Colton walked over to her and mimicked the pose her daughter just vacated.

"So many times over the last two weeks I wanted to ask you," he said solemnly, "but Mallory thought it would be best if we waited and didn't give you too much time to think about it." He gave her a lopsided grin and she couldn't help but return it. "If you really don't want to do it this way, we don't have to, but you should know that it would mean the world to both your kids and me if we did this tonight."

It was crazy how much she wanted to say yes – how excited it made her to think that in just a matter of a few short hours, she could be Mrs. Colton Hale.

She had the big wedding the first time – over a hundred guests, the big white gown, the half-dozen bridesmaids. There hadn't been much time to plan because she was pregnant, but it was stressful and the day itself was a bit of a blur. But to do this – to simply walk out of this room and up the makeshift aisle in the living room with Sam and Mallory there to witness it seemed like the most perfect wedding anyone could ask for.

"Let's do it," she said and laughed when Colton's eyes went wide.

"Really? You're sure?"

"I've never been more sure of anything in my life. I love you and I don't want to wait another day to be married to you."

And with a little hoot of delight, he wrapped his arms around her and swung her around. "You have no idea how happy you've made me!"

Once she was back on her feet, she kissed him soundly. "Yes, I do. Because that's exactly how happy you've made me."

"Susannah..."

But she didn't have any more time to talk. Grasping his shoulders, she spun him around and gave him a gentle shove toward the door. "Okay, you can't see me until the ceremony! I've got too much to do! Send Mallory back here! And Shelby! Oh, and if Georgia's here, send her back too! I have a feeling I'm going to need all the help I can get!"

Chuckling, Colton stopped at the door, his hand on the

knob, and turned to look at her. "The only thing you need to do is meet me in the living room. I'll be the one grinning like a loon as I stand next to Pastor Steve."

With her hand over her heart, she shook her head. "I love you, Colton."

"Love you too, beautiful."

———

"Are you nervous? Because...you should know...it's completely okay to be nervous. It's natural, really. Normal."

Colton nodded.

"I mean, no one would blame you. After all, it's your wedding day and you just found out about it a few hours ago." He paused. "So really, there's no shame in being nervous."

Colton chuckled softly as he turned his head. "Jake? Are you nervous?"

If anything, Jake seemed to pale slightly. "How could you *not* be nervous? I've had over a year to think about this and then a few weeks to seriously plan it. You've had... what...an hour?"

"Almost two," he corrected. "But it wouldn't matter if I had a year, two years, or two hours. I've been ready to marry Susannah almost since we met."

"Yeah, well..."

Reaching over, Colton rested his hand on Jake's shoulder. "It's not a competition and you're allowed to be as nervous or as mellow as you want. This is your day and you can feel however you want."

"It's your day too," Jake reminded him.

And for the first time since the topic was brought up a few weeks ago, it hit Colton just how much his friend was willing to sacrifice for him. Clearing his throat, he said, "I want you to know how much this means to me – you being willing to share this day with me and Susannah." He paused. "It was completely selfless and..."

Jake held up a hand to stop him. "You know, when Sam told me his idea, the first thought that came to me was how I wished I thought of it." He shook his head. "Mallory and Susannah are so close – sometimes they're more like sisters or best friends rather than mother and daughter."

Colton agreed.

"When I got home that day and told Mallory about the whole thing, she screamed with excitement and was so loud I thought for sure all the neighbors heard her," he said with a laugh. "But once it was out there, she was one hundred percent on board. I don't think she would have taken no for an answer today."

"Luckily Susannah didn't need to be convinced too much." He let out a long breath, looked toward the entryway and almost willed Susannah to be standing there waiting. Instead, Pastor Steve walked into the room and greeted guests on his way toward Jake and Colton. After shaking both their hands, he took his place at the front of the room – Jake to his right, Colton to his left.

"Gentlemen, it takes a lot to surprise me these days, and when I arrived and Shelby told me the change of plans, I have to admit I was genuinely surprised. I've never done a double wedding before," Steve said with a sincere smile. "But I can't think of a more special way to celebrate both couples and to ring in the new year."

"Thank you," both Colton and Jake said as they took their own places.

The original plan was to have the ceremony out on the deck and use heat lamps to keep everyone warm. But the temperature was near freezing so they decided at the last minute to set up everything in the house while still keeping some tables and chairs – and heat lamps – out on the deck for anyone who wanted to get some air after the ceremony. The massive living room was decorated with tons of garland made of evergreen and covered in white twinkly lights. It had the feel of being outside while keeping everyone warm.

All of the furniture had been removed and replaced with white chairs – fifty of them – and each of them was filled with family and friends. There were close to fifty people in all, but the only one Colton saw was Susannah. She stepped into the entryway with her arm looped through her son's – who had his sister on his other side – and Colton had never seen a more beautiful example of love.

Sam slowly made his way up the aisle between his mother and sister, and Colton knew he'd never forget this moment for as long as he lived.

There was a moment of mild confusion once everyone was standing in front of Pastor Steve, but once Sam kissed his mother and then his sister, everyone seemed to find their space.

With a smile, he began to speak. "You may not know this, but one of my greatest joys as a pastor is the honor of officiating weddings. Every wedding is as different as it is special, but I will never forget the first wedding I ever performed. I had the honor of officiating for a couple of dear friends. The groom was my best friend from college. I think I was the one who was most nervous out of the two of us."

Everyone laughed softly.

"Whether I know the couple personally or not doesn't change the joy I feel out of watching a couple coming together in holy matrimony. But I'm not going to lie to you, I think this wedding is going to be my new favorite because

I'm standing here with four of the most wonderful people I've ever met. I'm proud to call all of you friends and I thank you for including me in this special day. And I just know that Ezekiel is positively beaming as he looks down on us today. Nothing would have made him happier than seeing all the love in this one room."

They all nodded.

Then he straightened and opened his Bible. "Everyone ready?"

The four of them – as well as everyone in the room – let out another laugh.

"Dearly beloved, we are gathered here today for a most joyous occasion," Steve began. "Today we have the honor of witnessing and celebrating the joining of two wonderful couples." He paused and smiled at the four of them. "As most of you know, the decision to make this a double cere- mony happened rather last minute, but I am honored to be the one officiating over it today."

Colton gently squeezed Susannah's hand and looked at her with a smile. "You look beautiful," he mouthed, mindful not to interrupt the pastor's speech.

"Thank you," she mouthed in return.

"Jacob...Mallory, I understand the two of you have prepared your vows."

They nodded. "We have."

Susannah's eyes went wide and Colton knew exactly what she was thinking – they did not have vows prepared – not that he was worried. He knew when the time came, he would simply say what was in his heart.

"Jacob," Pastor Steve prompted.

Jake seemed to take a steadying breath as he turned to face Mallory. "Mallory Westbrook, it's been a long road to get us to the altar, but I treasure the journey. We were friends for a long time and then we became so much more. The years we spent apart..." his voice cracked, "were some of the roughest years of my life. I never dreamed that we'd get a second chance, but once you came back to Magnolia, I knew I couldn't let you go a second time. You are my love, my life, my everything. I love you." He slid the ring onto Mallory's finger.

"Mallory," the pastor prompted.

Colton looked over and saw the big smile on Mallory's face and even if she didn't utter a single word, he knew everyone in that room could tell how much she loved Jake.

"If anyone would have told fourteen-year-old me that one day I'd be standing here marrying Jake Summerford, well...I would have believed them," Mallory said with a sweet laugh. "I had no idea how that was going to happen, but in my heart, I always knew you were the one for me. I love the memories we've made and I look forward to all the ones still to come and I am so thankful that I finally get to be your wife. I love you." She slid the ring onto Jake's finger.

"Colton."

Show time...

"I remember the first time I came here to the house to do some work for Ezekiel. You came out to greet me and I swore I couldn't breathe. You smiled at me as you walked down those front steps and I remember thinking 'That's her. She's my forever.'" Smiling, he shook his head. "Of course, I was a little shy and more than a bit nervous to ask you out, but I've never been so glad for stepping out of my comfort zone. You are my hope, Susannah. You are everything that is good in the world and I am the luckiest man to be able to call you my wife." He let out a shaky breath as he prepared to slide the ring onto her finger. "Everything that has ever happened to me before brought me here to you. I love you."

Susannah stared down at the ring on her finger and looked up at him with tears in her eyes.

"Susannah."

Squeezing his hands slightly, she smiled. "Colton Hale, there aren't enough words to describe what you mean to me. I thought my life was all it was ever going to be – I had my children and a new business and I swore it was enough. Then you showed up here to do some work for my grandfather and for the first time in far too long, I knew I wanted something more. You have given me so much joy and love and laughter and so many things that I didn't even believe I deserved. You are my everything and I thank you for not giving up on me." She slid the ring onto his finger and smiled at him. "And I love you so much."

Colton wanted to pull her close and kiss her right in that moment but knew he had to wait for the pastor to tell them when.

"It gives me great pleasure to pronounce you...man and wife," he said to Jake and Mallory. "And...man and wife," he said to Colton and Susannah. "Gentlemen, you may kiss your brides!"

He moved in close and cupped Susannah's face gently in his hands before claiming her lips. She tasted so sweet and she was so precious to him – he still couldn't believe she was his.

They did it.

They were married.

And he was more than ready for their happily ever after.

They broke apart and rested their heads against each other. "You're the most beautiful bride I've ever seen," he whispered.

Blushing, she said, "Thank you. And you're the most handsome groom I've ever seen."

"Oh yeah?"

She nodded.

"Come on, you two!" Mallory cried. "We've got a party to start!" She and Jake made their way up the aisle.

"You ready for this?" Susannah asked.

"Sweetheart, I was ready the moment I first saw you. This is just the icing on the cake." He kissed her again before securing her arm through his and walking with her up the aisle.

To their party.

To their future.

EPILOGUE

"This is amazing."

"It certainly is."

"I don't think we'll ever be able to top it."

"Well, that doesn't mean we can't try."

"We should make this an annual thing."

Laughing, Colton finished rubbing sunscreen onto his wife's back. She had surprised him by wearing a bikini today and he didn't want her getting a sunburn. They were finally on their honeymoon and he was determined to make it the best trip possible for her.

"That could be arranged," he finally agreed. "But considering neither of us has traveled much, maybe we should try some new places too."

Lying on her stomach on the lounge chair, she shook her head. "All I'm saying is why mess with perfection? St. Thomas is clearly a hit – our own private villa with a pool, the beautiful beach only a couple of yards away, and room service. I'm telling you – I'd sell the inn and move here if I could."

Stretching out on the lounge beside her, he shook his

head. "Let's not get too far ahead of ourselves. Just promise you'll be open to vacationing in different places in the future. We can try a cruise, or maybe the Florida Keys, or even the West Coast or Mexico. Nothing too far away, but places neither of us have ever seen before. We can explore together."

Turning her head, she looked at him. "I like the sound of that."

"Me too."

She was silent for several minutes. "You know, for a while there I was upset that we had to wait to take this trip."

"Well, the inn has been booked almost every night since we opened. Then we had to hire a staff to help out and know they were competent enough to cover for you. We're lucky we were even able to get away now."

"I know. And then I was worried that I wouldn't be able to fully relax and enjoy myself but...I'm glad I was wrong."

Reaching over, he caressed her arm. "It's a tough job keeping you distracted, but I think I'm pretty good at it."

"Colton Hale, you are absolutely the best at it. Trust me."

"So what should we do tonight? You want to go out to eat or have dinner brought here to the villa?"

"Is it wrong that I want to eat in again? I find I'm really enjoying sitting out here by the pool by candlelight."

"There's nothing wrong with that and you deserve to be pampered and waited on."

Susannah rolled onto her side so she could fully face him. "We're not only on this trip for me. I want you to be able to do some of the things that you want."

"Sweetheart, being able to sit and relax with you has been a real treat. I think we both deserve some time to be a little lazy, don't you think?"

"Maybe..."

"You know we're going to hit the ground running as soon as we get home. With Mallory finding out she's pregnant and Sam and Shelby setting a wedding date, things are going to be crazy in the next several months. Soak up the peace and quiet now while we can."

"I have to admit, getting all of us back to Magnolia Sound was the best thing my grandfather ever did. It was like he knew it was where we would all find our happily ever afters."

It was hard not to agree. "Your grandfather was very astute and I'm forever thankful for him. I just wish he could have seen all the ways his gifts and his wisdom blessed this family."

"He knows," she said softly. "And soon, another whole generation will be here to carry on the traditions he started."

"That's what life is all about."

She smiled. "And I can't wait for us to experience it all together – more weddings, grandbabies, all of it."

The thought of having all those things – things he never thought he'd have – were enough to choke him up. "And it's all because of you," he said gruffly. "I'm incredibly blessed and it's all because you came into my life."

"We came into each other's lives," she corrected. "And all the befores, all our nows, and all our tomorrows...this life we have is precious and I never want us to take them for granted."

"Never," he vowed as he leaned forward and kissed her. Slowly. Sweetly.

When they broke apart, Susannah stood and looked around their private courtyard before giving him a sassy grin. "You know I never traveled before, right?"

He nodded.

"And you know I haven't worn a bikini since high school..."

Another nod.

Reaching behind her, she tugged on the ties of the bikini top before taking it off completely. "I also never skinny dipped. Care to join me?"

He almost fell and broke his leg in his haste to get up and whip off his shorts.

Susannah breezed by him and dove gracefully into their pool. Her bikini bottoms landed at his feet a moment later.

"Woman, you're going to be the death of me," he growled playfully, but still dove in after her.

Hell, he'd follow her anywhere.

Now and forever.

And Then One Day

COURTNEY BAKER IS ready to put small town life—and the man she can't have—behind her. Years of secretly crushing on her best friend's older brother have led nowhere and she's finally ready to move on. It would have been a great plan had she not drunkenly blurted out all her feelings and kissed him. At least she'll be able to forget all about it when she leaves town in less than 48 hours.

It takes a lot to surprise Dean Jones, but a kiss from the girl he's been secretly attracted to for years does just that. All it takes it one kiss for him to realize he doesn't want to let her go. But she's his sister's best friend and that's a line he knows he should never cross. Never mind that she seems determined to leave their small town—and him—behind.

When a storm and a broken car stop Courtney from leaving town, Dean sees perfect opportunity to get her out of his system. But can one night ever be enough?

CHAPTER 1

"You KNOW it's not going to be so bad."

"Yes, it is and you're the worst best friend ever."

Rolling her eyes, Courtney Baker leaned over and rested her head on her best friend Scarlett's shoulder. "I think the pregnancy hormones are making you more and more ridiculous every day. When is this baby coming?"

Sighing, Scarlett replied, "Not soon enough. We've got another ten weeks."

"Ugh, poor Mason."

Shoving her away, Scarlett cried, "Poor Mason? How about poor me? I'm the one whose emotions are all over the damn place! I swear, I cry at the drop of a hat!"

"You've been doing that practically since this baby was conceived. We're all used it by now."

"Well I'm not and the fact that you're moving so far away isn't helping."

Yeah, she knew this was going to be an issue–particularly the timing–but Courtney knew if she didn't do this now, she never would.

"Scar, we've been talking about this for months now. You know it's something I have to do."

"Oh, please. You've been threatening to move for years! Why did you wait until I was about to have a baby to do it? And you know you don't have to move right now. You don't have a job waiting for you, so what's the rush? Can't you wait until after my little peanut is born?"

"I thought we were calling him a bean?"

"And I thought I told you that no one knows the sex of the baby yet so ixnay-on-the-him-ay."

"We've got to get this baby out of you," Courtney said blandly. "It's like I don't even know who you are anymore. No one says ixnay at our age so...stop that."

And then the worst thing happened.

Scarlett started to cry.

Like...ugly cry.

"Oh, God...oh, no...just...I'm sorry! I didn't mean to upset you!" She muttered a curse and reached across the table for a napkin and quickly began wiping her friend's face. "Dammit, you have *got* to stop being so sensitive!"

No sooner were the words out of her mouth than Mason, Scarlett's fiancé, was right there beside them, his attention fully on Scarlett. "Hey," he said softly, "What's going on? There's no crying tonight. It's our wedding rehearsal party and only smiling is allowed." He kissed the tip of her nose before looking over at Courtney. "Everything okay here?"

"She's upset over the move again."

"Ah. Well, you have to admit, the timing's not the greatest," he replied.

"I know, but...for me, this is the way it has to be and she's going to have to understand. It's not my fault that Dr.

Curtis had to retire abruptly and there are no other dental practices local who are hiring. I need to work, Mason."

He gave her a patient smile. "I know, but you have to understand how hard this is on Scarlett. The wedding's tomorrow, the house we're building is behind schedule, and the pregnancy's really kicking her butt..."

"I am right here," Scarlett interrupted, looking first at Mason and then to Courtney. "You know you don't have to move so far away to find a job, Court, and it's not like you have to find something right this second. Why not take a couple of weeks and look some more?"

With a weary sigh, she looked at Mason and said, "Can you...give us a minute?"

Nodding, he kissed Scarlett before standing and walking away.

"What's so secretive that you can't say it in front of Mason? You know I'm just going to tell him whatever it is later, right?"

"And that's fine, but..." She groaned. "Okay, here it is. You know how my folks have always been into paranormal hunting?"

"Yeah..."

Another sigh. "Well...they've both taken some extended vacation time to go on some sort of cross-country trip with a group they belong to."

"O-kay. I still don't see what this has to do with you moving away though."

"When I lost my job and realized the best thing for me to do was move, they decided to list the house as an Airbnb for the time they're away as a source of income."

"What? But..."

"That means I don't have a place to live for the next

three months. They leave on Monday which is when I need to be out as well."

"Is that all?" Scarlett said, suddenly all smiles.

"Uh, yeah. It's kind of a big deal. I'm going to be homeless on top of already being jobless, sooo..."

"So stay at my place! You know we haven't decided what to do with it yet and it's just been sitting vacant for months! This is perfect! Now you can stay and..."

Courtney held up a hand to stop her. "Scar, I appreciate the offer, but I can't do it. I really..." She looked around the room and spotted one of the main reasons she was opting to move away. Forcing her attention back to Scarlett, she continued. "It's just time for me to have a fresh start someplace that isn't Magnolia Sound. I can't do small town life anymore. I just can't."

Tears began to well up again in Scarlett's eyes but Courtney wasn't having it.

"And you can*not* keep crying to get your way," she said with a small laugh. Jumping to her feet, she looked down at her friend and grinned. "This is going to be a good thing for me and you should be happy! Now if you'll excuse me, I'm going to grab a glass of wine."

Walking across the room, Courtney smiled and waved to people she knew but did her best to get to the bar as quickly as possible. Once there, she smiled at the bartender. "Moscato, please." Once she had her glass in hand, she thanked him and walked out onto the back deck of the Magnolia on the Sound–the new B&B that Mason's aunt owned. The house was over a hundred years old and recently renovated and it was quite possibly the most magnificent house she'd ever been in.

The weather was a little cool and she wished she had

grabbed a sweater, but...it was peaceful outside and the perfect spot for a little quiet reflection.

Leaning on the railing, she looked out at the Sound as she sipped her wine. She'd never admit it to anyone, but she really loved it here. Not the B&B–although it was beautiful–but the small coastal town where she'd lived her whole life. She loved the beach and her friends and family, but...nothing was happening for her here. Not only was her job gone, but she hadn't had a date in months and the men she did want to date–or rather, the *man* she wanted to date–was off limits.

And it sucked.

If it weren't for the fact that the dentist she was working for had to retire immediately therefore leaving her unemployed, she probably wouldn't have opted to move away. But considering the downward spiral her life was currently in, it seemed only logical to pick up and move someplace new and start over.

But yeah, the timing did suck.

She wanted to see Scarlett get married and luckily she was, but the thought of not being here when her best friend had her baby was a little harder to deal with. They had always talked about having their kids close together and hoping they'd be best friends too.

Hard to happen when no man has even attempted to touch me in almost six months...

That depressing thought had her taking a long drink of her wine and was thankful no one was there to witness her practically guzzling the whole thing down.

"Hey, Court."

Or so she thought.

Turning, she saw Scarlett's brother Kyle walking her way. He was super sweet, a total flirt, and completely harmless. There was zero attraction between the two of them and she considered him to be a good friend.

"Hey, yourself. Having fun?"

Standing beside her, he leaned against the railing as well and stared out at the beach. "I know this is just supposed to be a casual dinner after the whole wedding rehearsal, but I swear Mason's mother has me feeling like I'm a kid trying to sneak a spot at the grownup table." Chuckling, he shook his head. "You know my family's not fancy like the Bishops. This just all feels a little weird. Why couldn't we just have a cookout in the backyard at home or something?"

Turning her head, she looked at him and laughed. "Kyle, can you imagine the sophisticated Bishop family hanging out in your dad's backyard? Come on!" Then she motioned toward the inside of the massive house. "And are you telling me you're not enjoying the food here? The menu has been spectacular! I'm already planning on putting about a dozen crab cakes in my purse for later."

"Classy," he said, still laughing. They stood in companionable silence for several moments. "So I hear you're moving to Raleigh."

She nodded. "Yup."

"Why so far?"

"It's only three hours away."

"You know my sister is freaking out over it though, right?"

"Yeah, I know," she said sadly, her eyes never leaving the waves crashing on the shore. The sun was going down and it was her favorite time of day. "Once the baby's born, she won't even notice I'm gone."

"Somehow, I doubt that."

But it wasn't Kyle who spoke, but his older brother Dean.

As in...the man she wanted most in the world and couldn't have.

Why did he have to come out here? I specifically came out here to escape!

Both Courtney and Kyle turned and looked at him and she did her best to appear calm and cool—and not at all like her heart was ready to beat right out of her chest at the sight of him.

Tall, shaggy dark hair, blue eyes, and dimples. Honestly, every time she was near him her ovaries sighed. It was so unfair that he was off-limits.

Smiling at her, Dean raised his beer as he commented, "It doesn't matter how much time my sister spends with the baby, nothing can replace a best friend."

And he was sweet too, damn him.

When he continued to stare at her expectantly, she realized she probably should respond. "Nah. I think between the baby, Mason, and everyone coming to see the baby, Scarlett's going to be just fine. And it's not like I'm moving to another country or anything, I'm only a few hours away."

"Still not the same," he said mildly before looking at his younger brother. "Can you believe our baby sister is getting married tomorrow?"

Kyle shrugged. "Considering she's just about ready to give birth, I'm kind of happy she's getting married tomorrow." He winked at Courtney. "Am I right?"

"Look, I firmly believe in the institution of marriage," she said evenly, "but it's not like they *had* to get married. No one has to do that anymore."

"Still," Kyle replied, "I just think it's the right thing to do."

"What is this, 1950?" Dean asked with a small laugh.

"On that note, I'm going to get a refill," she said, stepping away from the railing and raising her glass. "I'll see you two later." She sashayed away and got a brief whiff of Dean's cologne—all fresh, clean, and masculine—and she wanted to rub up against him and just inhale deeply.

Yeah, it was definitely time for another drink.

Maybe two.

As she made her way back toward the bar, she caught a server walking by with those mini crab cakes she loved so much and grabbed a few. At the bar, she had her glass refilled while she noshed and then caught another server who had a tray of chicken satay. So she grabbed some of them as well. She figured if she was going to slam back some cocktails, it would be smart to keep eating.

Out of the corner of her eye she spotted Dean walking back into the room with Kyle and sighed.

It wasn't fair. She'd been crushing on him since she was fifteen and because he was six years older, it was completely inappropriate. Now? Not so much. But he was her best friend's brother and as such, that meant Dean was completely off-limits. There had never been a conversation between her and Scarlett regarding this—mainly because she was too embarrassed to admit how she felt. For some reason, Courtney felt her friend wouldn't have a big problem if she had crushed on Kyle or even Hunter because they were closer in age. Dean was...well...not only was there a bigger age-gap, but he was way more serious and level-headed than his brothers. He didn't do casual relationships and for a long time, Courtney wasn't looking for anything long-term.

A fact Scarlett would have brought up as a way of discouraging this crush.

Too bad it didn't work.

No matter how many times she told it to herself.

Dean Jones was the ultimate man to her and she knew the main reason she never wanted a serious relationship was because he was always right there–small town living meant they ran into each other a lot. And every time she saw him, it just reinforced why no other man measured up and how it was never going to happen for them.

And now she had to move on with her life.

He caught her eye from across the room and smiled. The weak smile she gave him was forced and rather than think about it, she turned her attention back to the bar and ordered a second glass of wine.

Everything felt...off.

Glancing around the room, Dean Jones saw how everyone was laughing and smiling and having a great time and yet...he felt like he didn't belong.

No, that wasn't it; he felt envious.

And how pathetic was that?

His baby sister was getting ready to have a baby and was getting married in the morning. She was six years younger than him. He glanced over at his brother Hunter who was two years younger than Dean and already had a kid. Granted, Hunter and his on-again-off-again girlfriend never married, but they had started a family. Kyle was next and wasn't in any kind of relationship so there wasn't anything there, but...dammit, Dean felt like his family was passing him by.

Frowning, he took a pull of his beer and continued to scan the room. He knew everyone here–literally, everyone. True, this was an intimate dinner for thirty, but he knew each and every face here. That came with living in a small town. As he continued to look around, he realized they were all doing things with their lives like getting married and having kids, or for the older couples, they were traveling and enjoying their grandkids. And where was he? Nowhere, with no one and no prospects of there being a someone.

Yeah, pathetic.

He caught a glimpse of Courtney from across the room and realized they were the only two people in the room who didn't look like they were having any fun. Dean knew why he wasn't, but was curious about why she wasn't. If there was one thing he knew about Courtney, it was how she liked having a good time. She was usually the life of the party–always loud and boisterous and full of laughter.

She's certainly not doing any of those things right now...

Maybe the fact that she was days away from moving was distracting her, but damn, he wished she didn't look so sad and alone. He was about to go over and talk to her but quickly decided against it. She never seemed to have a problem laughing and joking with Kyle or even Hunter, but whenever he was around, she usually clammed up.

Or walked away like she had back out on the deck.

It was probably because while they were all growing up, he had to be like one of the parents–always watching his younger siblings while his father was at work and making sure no one got into trouble. It was a lot of responsibility on him and he took it seriously.

Especially when his mother died.

After that happened, he was even more protective of his family and tried to fill the void of losing their mom.

So he was the serious brother, the rule enforcer, and...it sucked.

Before he could think any more about it, the announcement that dinner was being served was called out. He took his place at a table along with his brothers, father, grandfather, and...Courtney.

Smiling, he held out a chair for her and she softly thanked him. Taking the seat beside her, he thought maybe it was prophetic that she was sitting with them. They could talk and he could try to figure out why she was being so quiet.

And maybe he'd finally be brave enough to...

"There you are," Scarlett said as she came walking over. She grabbed Courtney's hand and pulled her to her feet. "I want you sitting with me up at the head table. Sam and Shelby are sitting with us too, so..." Then she looked at her brothers and smiled. "Sorry for making this the lone guy table, but..."

"Or maybe we should call it the lonely guy table," Kyle joked and Hunter punched him in the arm. "Ow!"

"No worries, little miss," their grandfather said, ignoring the spectacles beside him. "Although, I was looking forward to having such a beautiful girl sitting with us."

"Oh, stop, Tommy. You rascal," Courtney said before walking over and planting a loud, smacking kiss on his grandfather's cheek. "You better save a dance for me tomorrow!"

"You know it!" he called out and Dean swore the old guy was blushing.

Before he could even process where Courtney was going, their meals were being served. Conversation around the table flowed and once everyone was done eating, speeches were made by both Scarlett and Mason—thanking everyone for coming and to talk about how excited they both were for the wedding tomorrow. Honestly, Dean was happy for them. Never in a million years did he imagine his sister marrying into one of the wealthiest families in town, but he knew that had little to do with their relationship. Still, he was happy that Scarlett would hopefully never have to struggle again.

They'd done that enough while growing up.

He raised his glass with everyone to toast the happy couple, he enjoyed a celebratory cupcake when they were passed around, and was more than a little thankful that the night was coming to an end. Tomorrow would be even longer and, no doubt, more draining, and right now the only thing Dean was looking forward to was going home and enjoying a little peace and quiet before going to sleep.

Yeah, just call me Mr. Excitement...

Walking across the room, he wanted a chance to say goodnight to Scarlett and Mason. As he got closer, however, he could see his sister looked upset.

Again.

Damn pregnancy hormones. He swore his sister had cried more in the last seven months than she had in her entire life.

When he was beside her, he carefully asked, "Hey, what's going on? What are you upset about now?"

Mason was the one to answer. "Scarlett feels like Courtney had a little too much to drink and is worried about her driving home and...let's just say things got a little tense."

"Dean," Scarlett began pitifully, "you have to make sure she doesn't drive! She won't listen to me and I realize she doesn't have far to go, but...you have to go after her! She's probably still in the driveway. It's a little chaotic even with the hired valet and..."

"Isn't she sleeping by you tonight?" he quickly interrupted before she got herself even more worked up. "I thought that was the plan–Courtney was staying with you at your place."

"She is, but she's mad at me and said she's not staying over!" she sobbed. "How could she do that? She's my maid of honor and...and..."

Dean looked at her and then Mason before he nodded. "Okay, okay, don't worry. I'll make sure she safely gets to your place." Then he paused. "Wait, when we say your place, do we mean your old place or your place on the beach–Mason's place?"

"The place on the beach is *our* place," Scarlett corrected. "But yeah, I mean my old place. We wanted one last night to hang out there like old times, and now she said she changed her mind!"

And she was crying again.

"I've got this," he said firmly. Shaking Mason's hand, he added, "Take care of her and I'll...I'll deal with Court."

"Thanks, man."

With a quick kiss on Scarlett's cheek, Dean made his way across the room and out to the large entryway while trying to find Courtney. He hadn't seen her leave, but that didn't mean she hadn't stopped to talk to anyone on her way out.

"You leaving too?" Hunter asked when he spotted him in the foyer.

"Uh, yeah. Have you seen Courtney?"

"I think I saw her go out the back door. How come?"

Dean quickly relayed the situation before excusing himself and walking back through the house. With no other choice, he stepped outside and headed down the to the yard. Several people were still milling around and he scanned the property to try to figure out where she went.

A lone figure on the pier caught his eye.

Courtney.

Her shoulders were hunched and shaking and he knew she was crying. With a muttered curse, he started walking across the yard and down the pier. When he got to her side, he stood there and looked out at the Sound like she was.

"You want to talk about it?" he quietly asked.

"Not particularly."

Her words were spoken so softly he could barely hear her. Turning his head to look at her, he wasn't sure what to say.

"I don't need a babysitter, Dean," she said after a minute. "You don't have to stand here and watch over me. I'm not a kid anymore."

Like I haven't noticed...

He laughed softly. "Yeah, I got that, Court, but you know you're not in any condition to drive, so..." And he braced himself for the fight that was sure to come. "Scarlett's just worried about you. You know that. So why don't you let me drive you home and we'll get Kyle or Hunter to bring your car to you, okay?"

She looked up at him and his mouth went dry. It wasn't the first time he noticed how beautiful Courtney was—it was something that hit him years ago—but it was the first time he was seeing the vulnerability in her. For once, she wasn't the sassy, confident girl she presented to the world.

And he had no idea how to react.

"I wasn't going to drive. I know better than that." She gently swiped her hand over her cheek to wipe away the tears and he wished he had a handkerchief or something to offer her. "I'm more upset because she didn't need to humiliate me like that in front of everyone. Hell, she could have just offered to let me drive home with her, but instead, she practically shouts it out for everyone that I've had four glasses of wine!"

A small laugh escaped and she shot him an angry glare.

"Okay, yeah, that was wrong of her, but you know Scarlett's all over the place right now. We've talked about this. So maybe she could have handled it different, but...let's be honest, Court, you're possibly making a bigger deal out of it than it was too."

And then he held his breath and waited for her to argue with him.

But she didn't.

"Everything's changing," she said, her gaze turning back to the water. "There's a part of me that knows it's all for the better–Scarlett's happy, the baby will be here before we all know it, and she's found this amazing love with Mason." She paused. "Then there's me. I'm unemployed, my parents are off chasing ghosts and turning our home into an Airbnb which leaves me homeless come Monday morning, and I'm moving to a city where I literally know no one." She shook her head. "I didn't mean to ruin her night."

Unable to help himself, Dean put his arm around her and hugged her.

And she instantly stiffened beside him.

Trying not to focus on that, he did his best to encourage her. "I know things all seem bleak right now, but you have to believe it's going to get better. I've been hearing you tell everyone how you much you hate living in a small town so... here's your big chance to find someplace that's a better fit for you. And...you know you'll always have a place here. Even if it's not with your folks, Scarlett would always welcome you home whenever you want."

"I know that..."

"But...?"

"But...it's not the same. Everyone's moving forward and I'm just...I'm not. This whole job thing is making me crazy. I mean why did I have to lose my job now?"

"To be fair, Dr. Curtis was like a hundred years old. He didn't exactly instill confidence when you went in for a cleaning."

She chuckled. "First of all, he's only seventy-five, but yeah, he did look a lot older." She sighed. "I just wish he would have sold the practice rather than just closing his doors. He's been my family dentist since I was a kid–and everyone else's dentist here in town! How could he just leave like that? It's like he didn't even care about all the patients who now have to scramble to find a new dentist or his employees who need to search for new jobs!"

"I'm sure you're not going to have any problem finding a new job," he said, hoping he sounded optimistic. "I thought dental hygienists were always in big demand."

"Not in small towns," she murmured, stepping out of his embrace. Turning around, she faced him, and Dean noticed she didn't look quite as sad as she had a moment ago. "It's just another sucky aspect of my life! I was the youngest hygienist in the office–everyone else had been with him since forever! Most of them are retiring! And so here I am with no job and no prospects and I have to move across the state and hope I find something!"

"So...wait," he said, holding up a hand to her. "Why are you moving if you don't have a job yet? Shouldn't you find the job first and then move?"

"There are a lot of jobs in the Raleigh area so I figured it would be a safe place to start. I'm going to stay at one of those extended-stay hotels while I job hunt and then I'll find an apartment. It's not ideal but with my parents renting out the house to strangers, I had to get creative with what I'm doing."

"Wow, Court, I had no idea. I'm really sorry."

She shrugged. "Yeah, well...this is my life. Nothing goes my way and no one wants me, so..." She gasped before covering her mouth and turning her back on him.

No one wants her? What the...? Wait, did she mean her folks or did she mean...?

For some stupid reason, he needed clarification–knew he'd go crazy if he didn't know specifically what she was talking about.

Stepping around her so he was facing her, he asked, "What do you mean no one wants you? That's crazy! Your parents are just doing their own thing right now. They probably thought it wouldn't be a big deal to you."

Groaning loudly, Courtney spun around and started to walk away. "I'm going to call an Uber. I...I'll see you tomorrow."

He didn't let her go even three steps before he was in front of her again. "Hey, what's going on? What did I say?"

Her big green eyes stared up at him and he swore she was going to start crying again, but then...something changed. Her expression went from sad to neutral to something he couldn't quite define.

He saw her swallow hard before she seemed to pull herself together. "I wasn't talking about my parents, Dean. I'm talking about guys. Men! I haven't had a date in forever and no one in this town has any interest in me!"

"You're crazy. That's just not possible. I mean...look at you!" he said emphatically, motioning to her body–which right now was encased in a clingy sapphire blue cocktail dress. Her dark hair was blowing a bit wildly in the wind but she was still a beautiful woman.

Which is what he told her.

A snort of disbelief was her only response.

"Courtney, I'm serious! You are a beautiful woman and if the guys around here don't see it and don't appreciate it, then they're idiots!"

"Oh, really?" she asked, her voice dripping with sarcasm.

"Yeah, really."

"Then I guess that makes *you* one of the idiots," she grumbled before trying to walk away, but he stopped her.

"Excuse me?"

"You heard me. Then you're an idiot too. Probably the biggest idiot."

"Hey!" he snapped. "What the hell? What did I do?"

Her eyes were blazing with fire when she looked up at him and for the life of him, Dean had no idea why she was so pissed off at him.

"Because you're too blind to see this!" she said right before she snaked a hand around his nape and pulled his head down and kissed him.

Shock held Dean immobile for all of three seconds before he realized what was happening and then...holy crap.

He had no idea what he was expecting, but Courtney's kiss wasn't angry–like her words were getting–but it was soft and sensual.

He was the one to kick it up a notch.

Reaching up, his hands cupped her face as he dove in for more of her. She pressed closer and the feel of her curvy body pressed up against him from head to toe was enough to turn him on more than he'd been in years.

If ever.

And just as he shifted and let his hands skim over her

cheeks, her throat, her shoulders, and before his arms could wrap around her waist, she broke the kiss and looked at him in absolute horror.

"*Ohmygod*," she whispered right before she turned and ran.

For the second time in as many minutes, he was frozen in place. By the time his head was clear enough to think, she was out of sight–and out of the yard. Running across the yard, he spotted her in the driveway. As much as he didn't want to make a scene, he knew he had to call out to her, to stop her. Just as he was about to, Dean spotted his brother Kyle standing with her and ushering her toward his car.

"Son of a bitch," he hissed and immediately realized this was probably for the better. She'd had too much to drink, was upset, and would more than likely have no memory of ever kissing him come tomorrow morning.

Which was a damn shame.

Because there wasn't a doubt in his mind that he'd ever forget it.

Pre-Order
AND THEN ONE DAY
https://geni.us/AndThenOneDay

ALSO BY SAMANTHA CHASE

The Enchanted Bridal Series:

The Wedding Season

Friday Night Brides

The Bridal Squad

Glam Squad & Groomsmen

The Montgomery Brothers Series:

Wait for Me

Trust in Me

Stay with Me

More of Me

Return to You

Meant for You

I'll Be There

Until There Was Us

Suddenly Mine

A Dash of Christmas

The Shaughnessy Brothers Series:

Made for Us

Love Walks In

Always My Girl

This is Our Song

Sky Full of Stars

Holiday Spice

Tangled Up in You

Band on the Run Series:

One More Kiss

One More Promise

One More Moment

The Christmas Cottage Series:

The Christmas Cottage

Ever After

Silver Bell Falls Series:

Christmas in Silver Bell Falls

Christmas On Pointe

A Very Married Christmas

A Christmas Rescue

Christmas Inn Love

Life, Love & Babies Series:

The Baby Arrangement

Baby, Be Mine

Baby, I'm Yours

Preston's Mill Series:

Roommating

Speed Dating

Complicating

The Protectors Series:

Protecting His Best Friend's Sister

Protecting the Enemy

Protecting the Girl Next Door

Protecting the Movie Star

7 Brides for 7 Soldiers

Ford

7 Brides for 7 Blackthornes

Logan

Standalone Novels

Jordan's Return

Catering to the CEO

In the Eye of the Storm

A Touch of Heaven

Moonlight in Winter Park

Wildest Dreams

Going My Way

Going to Be Yours

Waiting for Midnight

Seeking Forever

Mistletoe Between Friends

Snowflake Inn

ABOUT SAMANTHA CHASE

Samantha Chase is a New York Times and USA Today bestseller of contemporary romance. She released her debut novel in 2011 and currently has more than sixty titles under her belt! When she's not working on a new story, she spends her time reading romances, playing way too many games of Scrabble or Solitaire on Facebook, wearing a tiara while playing with her sassy pug Maylene...oh, and spending time with her husband of 25 years and their two sons in North Carolina.

Where to Find Me:
Website: www.chasing-romance.com
Facebook: www.facebook.com/SamanthaChaseFanClub
Twitter: https://twitter.com/SamanthaChase3
Sign up for my mailing list and get exclusive content and chances to win members-only prizes!
https://www.chasing-romance.com/newsletter

Made in the USA
Middletown, DE
21 February 2020